# Madmen and Specialists

# MADMEN
# AND
# SPECIALISTS
A Play by Wole Soyinka

A Spotlight Dramabook
HILL AND WANG  ·  NEW YORK
A division of Farrar, Straus and Giroux

The first version of *Madmen and Specialists* was performed at the 1970 Playwrights' Workshop Conference at the Eugene O'Neill Theater Center, Waterford, Connecticut. The first complete version, printed here, had its première at the University of Ibadan, Nigeria, in March 1971, with the University Theatre Arts Company. The cast was as follows:

| | | |
|---|---|---|
| AAFAA | *Mendicants* | Femi Johnson |
| BLINDMAN | | Femi Osofisan |
| GOYI | | Wale Ogunyemi |
| CRIPPLE | | Tunji Oyelana |
| SI BERO *Sister to Dr. Bero* | | Deola Adedoyin |
| IYA AGBA | *Two old Women* | Nguba Agolia |
| IYA MATE | | Bopo George |
| DR. BERO *Specialist* | | Nat Okoro |
| PRIEST | | Gbenga Sonuga |
| THE OLD MAN *Bero's Father* | | Dapo Adelugba |

*Designed and directed by the author.*

The action takes place in and around the home clinic of Dr. Bero, lately returned from the wars.

# Part One

*(Open space before* BERO's *home and clinic. The clinic is down in a cellar. The level ground in the fore and immediate front space serve as drying space for assorted barks and herbs. The higher structure to one side is a form of semi-open hut. Inside it sit* IYA AGBA *and* IYA MATE. IYA AGBA *is smoking a thin pipe.* IYA MATE *stokes a small fire.*

*By the roadside is a group of mendicants—*CRIPPLE, GOYI, BLINDMAN *and* AAFAA. AAFAA's *St. Vitus spasms are designed to rid the wayfarer of his last pennies in a desperate bid to be rid of the sight.* GOYI *is held stiffly in a stooping posture by a contraption which is just visible above his collar. The* CRIPPLE *drags on his knees. They pass the time by throwing dice from the gourd rattle.*

*The* CRIPPLE *has just thrown the dice.)*

AAFAA

Six and four. Good for you.

CRIPPLE

Your turn, Blindman. *(Gives the dice and gourd to* BLINDMAN.*)*
*(*BLINDMAN *throws.)*

Five and five. Someone is going to give us fivers.

GOYI

Fat chance of that. *(He throws.)*

AAFAA

Three and two, born loser. What did you stake?

GOYI

The stump of the left arm.

CRIPPLE

Your last?

GOYI

No, I've got one left.

BLINDMAN

Your last. You lost the right stump to me yesterday.

GOYI

Do you want it now or later?

BLINDMAN

Keep it for now.

CRIPPLE

When do I get my eye, Aafaa?

AAFAA

Was it the right or the left?

GOYI

Does it matter?

AAFAA

Sure it does. If it's the right one he can take it out now. The left is my evil eye and I need it a while longer.

CRIPPLE

It was the right.

AAFAA

I've just remembered the right is my evil eye.

CRIPPLE

I'll make you an offer. Let me throw against both of you for Goyi's stumps. I'll stake the eye Aafaa lost to me.

GOYI

Why leave me out? I still want to try my luck.

BLINDMAN

You have nothing left to stake.

CRIPPLE

You're just a rubber ball, Goyi. You need a hand to throw with, anyway.

4

**GOYI**

I can use my mouth.

**AAFAA**

To throw dice? You'll eat sand, my friend.

**BLINDMAN**

Sooner or later we all eat sand.

**CRIPPLE**

Hey, you're beginning to sound like the Old Man.

**AAFAA** (*voice change*)

Did you eat sand, my friend? We'll make you the Ostrich in our touring circus.

**BLINDMAN**

The limbless acrobat will now perform his wonderful act—how to bite the dust from three classic positions.

**GOYI**

Upright, take off, and prone.

**CRIPPLE**

We'll never go on that tour.

**AAFAA**

Roll up—roll up. Presenting the Creatures of As in the timeless parade.

**BLINDMAN**

Think we'll ever make that tour?

**AAFAA**

We will. But until the millions start rolling in, we better not neglect the pennies. (*He nudges them, pointing to* SI BERO, *who approaches, carrying a small bag from which protrude some twigs with leaves and berries. The* MENDICANTS *begin their performance as soon as they sense her approach.* BLINDMAN *is alms collector,* GOYI *repeats a single acrobatic trick,* AAFAA *is the "dancer."* BLINDMAN *shakes the rattles while the* CRIPPLE *drums with his crutches and is lead singer.* BLINDMAN *collects alms in the rattles.*)

SI BERO (*as* AAFAA *moves to intercept her*)

Don't try that nonsense with me. I live in this neighbourhood, remember?

AAFAA

(*His spasms cease abruptly. The others also stop playing*).
Don't they say charity begins at home?

SI BERO

Your preaching is so good it's a wonder you can't find yourself a congregation.

AAFAA (*stiffening*)

What congregation, woman? Who said I was ever a preacher?

SI BERO

You were never anything. Go and find some decent work to do.

AAFAA

With this affliction of mine?

SI BERO

It comes and goes, not so? You can work in between.

AAFAA

And this one? And that? And that?
(*She points lastly to* GOYI.)
If it weren't for the iron rod holding up his spine he would collapse like a toad you step on. Just what sort of work do you want him to do?

GOYI

A penny or two, Si Bero. We haven't eaten today.

BLINDMAN

And that is God's truth. Aafaa, why do you pick a quarrel with her? Just ask her for a few pennies, you know she treats us well.

6

CRIPPLE

The lane is deserted. Nobody comes and goes any more.

GOYI

Something is driving them away from here. If there isn't something going on, then this isn't an iron I have in my back.

AAFAA

It is your neighbourhood, you say, Si Bero. What are you doing to drive people away?

SI BERO

Perhaps your mother's ghost is haunting the place. Why don't you ask her the next time she visits you?

AAFAA

Why do you always pick on me, old woman? What has my mother done to you?

SI BERO

She gave birth to you for a start.
(*She throws a penny to the* CRIPPLE *who tosses it into the gourd.*)
If you want more than that, you know where to come. I still need people to sort out my herbs.

AAFAA

Herbs! Herbs! Herbs! Always—come and sort out herbs to earn yourself a decent coin.

SI BERO

And eat. You can have work and eat. The two go together.
(*She goes out.*)

CRIPPLE (*throwing the coin in the gourd, calls after her*)
God bless you, Si Bero.

BLINDMAN

He shall, he will, he must.

GOYI

He'd better or I'll know the reason why.

CRIPPLE

Your turn, Aafaa.

AAFAA

What for?

CRIPPLE

A penny is something.

AAFAA

Not for me.

GOYI

Give her a pennyworth, then.

AAFAA

Can't be bothered.

BLINDMAN

Go on. Don't be mean.

CRIPPLE

You're the priest, after all.

AAFAA (*suddenly grinning*)

A penny's worth, you say?

CRIPPLE

That's only fair.

AAFAA (*shouting after the now distant woman*)

God bless your brother!
(*They all break out guffawing.*)

GOYI

More grease to his elbow.

AAFAA

Not forgetting his armpits.

8

BLINDMAN

More power to his swagger stick!

CRIPPLE

May light ever shine . . .

AAFAA

From his braids and buttons.

GOYI

May he come home safely . . .

AAFAA

To your loving arms.

CRIPPLE

Not to mention his Daddy's.

GOYI

God help her, that is some brother she has. You may say he is . . . dutiful.

CRIPPLE

Him a dutiful son? You're crazy.

BLINDMAN

I know what he means.
(*He points an imaginary gun.*)
Bang! All in the line of duty!
(GOYI *clutches his chest, slumps over.*)

AAFAA

Did we try him?

CRIPPLE

Resurrect, you fool. Nobody tried you yet.

AAFAA (*in a ringing voice*)

You are *accused.*

BLINDMAN

Satisfied?

CRIPPLE

Fair enough.

BLINDMAN

Bang!

(GOYI *slumps.*)

AAFAA (*rinsing his hands*)

Nothing to do with me.

BLINDMAN

Fair trial, no?

AAFAA

Decidedly yes.

BLINDMAN

What does he say himself?

GOYI

Very fair, gentlemen. I have no complaints.

BLINDMAN

In that case we permit you to be buried.

GOYI

You are generous, gentlemen. I have a personal aversion to vultures.

BLINDMAN

Oh, come come. Nice birds they are. They clean up after the mess.

CRIPPLE

Not like some bastards we know.

(*He spits.*)

AAFAA (*posing*)

In a way you may call us vultures. We clean up the mess made by others. The populace should be grateful for our presence.

(*He turns slowly round.*)

If there is anyone here who does not approve us, just say so and we quit.

(*His hand makes the motion of half-drawing out a gun.*)

I mean, we are not here because we like it. We stay at immense sacrifice to ourselves, our leisure, our desires, vocation, specialization, etcetera, etcetera. The moment you say, Go, we . . .

(*He gives another inspection all round, smiles broadly and turns to the others.*)

They insist we stay.

CRIPPLE

I thought they would. Troublesome little insects but . . . they have a sense of gratitude. I mean, after all we did for them.

GOYI

And still do.

BLINDMAN

And will continue to do.

CHORUS

Hear hear hear hear. Very well said, sir.

GOYI

Oh, come on. Shall we follow the woman or yap here all day? Let's get spying.

AAFAA

She's a devil, that's my complaint. She was born with a stone in her stomach.

GOYI

What's wrong? It's the job we are here to do, isn't it?

AAFAA

I still don't like messing about with her herbs.

BLINDMAN

Herbs are herbs, not so? Let's get going.

AAFAA

That woman's herbs are not just herbs. She hoards them and treats them like children. The whole house is full of twigs. If it's a straightforward business, why doesn't she use them? Or sell them or something?

GOYI

But everyone knows she's mad. They get that way after a while living alone. I've known one woman in my village who collects potsherds. Any piece of broken pot would do. Just let an old woman live by herself for a short while and she gets up to all sorts of things. Boxes, cupboards, trunks, every nook and corner. You couldn't walk on the floor without crunching pottery under your foot. Then she would scream curses at you.

CRIPPLE

What are we to do?

GOYI

There must be some way to stay nearer the house most of the day. We can't spend the whole day sorting herbs.

AAFAA

She's a witch. When she spirits out a foetus from the belly of a pregnant woman she pickles it in the herbs and it goes in a bottle for her brother's experiments.

BLINDMAN

For a so-called chaplain you talk plenty of nonsense.

AAFAA

Listen to the blind fool. What do you know about it?

CRIPPLE

Are we going to argue or follow her home?

GOYI

I don't like the whole business. She has been good to us.

12

AAFAA

With the pennies she throws as if she's feeding a dog? I spit on that kind of goodness!

CRIPPLE

I still don't like it. Why is he doing it? His own family too, what's he up to?

GOYI

He's a specialist.

AAFAA

Amen.

GOYI

What?

AAFAA

Amen. He is a specialist. That takes care of everything, not so?

GOYI

There is bound to be something in it for us.

BLINDMAN

Something like burnt fingers?

GOYI

What do you mean?

BLINDMAN (*shrugs*)

When things go wrong it's the lowest who get it first.

AAFAA

There is money at the bottom of it.

CRIPPLE

(*He places* BLINDMAN'*s hand on his shoulder and starts off in the direction of the house.*)

And we are at the bottom. So, let's go and make sure the woman doesn't stumble on any official secrets.

AAFAA (*checks*)

Rem Acu Tetigisti.

CRIPPLE

What? I don't get you.

AAFAA

R.A.T.! R.A.T.! I smell a rat.

GOYI

Is he having an attack?

CRIPPLE

What's up, Aafaa?

AAFAA

You said it yourself—Official Secrets. Official rat is what I smell. Yessir! We'll get paid something decent. Secret Service funds and all that. Let's celebrate.

GOYI

Nonsense. It's just a simple family vendetta.

AAFAA

Christ! Every one of you freaks will have ideas! And where did you pick up that word, anyway?

GOYI

Where you pick up yours, leave me alone.

AAFAA (*haughtily*)

One thing I disapproved of in the Old Man was he didn't discriminate. Talk of casting pearls before swine. Vendetta my foot. I tell you the Cripple has Rem Acu Tetigistied it. Official Secrets that's what's at the bottom of it. Bottomless account. We'll get overtime and risk allowance.

GOYI

It's not going to be risky, is it?

AAFAA

I know you have none, but I'll be risking my conscience. That needs compensation.

CRIPPLE

What do you think, Blindman?

BLINDMAN

Hm. Aafaa may be right. For once.

AAFAA

Never mind the cleverness. You agree.

BLINDMAN

R.A.T. You have touched the matter with a needle.

GOYI

Where? I'm still lost.

AAFAA

Where? I'll soon show you, dumbclod.
(*He lunges for* GOYI's *crotch.*)

GOYI (*protecting himself*)

No!

AAFAA

Why not? You got any more use for it?

BLINDMAN

Maybe he wants to continue the line.

AAFAA

What! This crooked line? It would be a disservice to humanity.

CRIPPLE

Hey. Think he'll do that to his own father?

BLINDMAN

When the Specialist wants results badly enough . . .

CRIPPLE

Yes, but what results?

AAFAA

Does it matter?
(*Voice change. He points a "needle" held low, at* GOYI.)
Say anything, say anything that comes into your head but
SPEAK, MAN!
(*He twists the needle upwards.* GOYI, *hand over crotch, yells.*)

BLINDMAN (*solemnly*)

Rem Acu Tetigisti.

AAFAA

Believe me, this hurts you more than it hurts me. Or—vice versa.
Truth hurts. I am a lover of truth. Do you find you also love
truth? Then let's have the truth. THE TRUTH!
(*He gives another push.* GOYI *screams.*)

CRIPPLE and BLINDMAN

Rem Acu Tetigisti.

AAFAA

Think not that I hurt you but that Truth hurts. We are all
seekers after truth. I am a Specialist in truth. Now shall we
push it up all the way, all the way? Or shall we have all the
truth all the truth.
(*Another push.* GOYI *screams, then his head slumps.*)
Hm, the poor man has fainted.

CRIPPLE and BLINDMAN

Rem Acu Tetigisti.
(AAFAA *makes a motion of slapping his face several times.* GOYI
*revives.*)

GOYI

Where am I?

16

CRIPPLE

Within the moment of truth, dear friend.

AAFAA (*chanting*)

Rem Acu . . .

OTHERS

Tetigisti, tetigisti.

ALTOGETHER

Rem Acu Tetigisti.

AAFAA

You have touched it with a . . .

OTHERS

Fine needle, fine fine needle.

ALL

You have touched it with a fine fine.

AAFAA

Rem Acu . . .

(*They repeat the song,* AAFAA *singing Rem Acu Tetigisti in counterpoint to the others* "You have touched it with a needle.")
Hey.
(*He taps* GOYI *on the shoulder.*)
Are you recovered? Good. Here we go again.

CRIPPLE

Perhaps he needs a drink of water.

AAFAA

Really? Well, give him one, then. We are no monsters here. No one will charge me with heartlessness. Give him a drink of water. A large one.

(BLINDMAN *hands* GOYI *a "bowl" of water.* GOYI *drains it while they all watch avidly.*)
Satisfied? Happy? More? No.
(*He takes the bowl and hands it to* BLINDMAN.)

Anything else? Perhaps you would like to use the conveniences?
The toilet?

(GOYI *nods.*)

Over there. Be my guest.
(GOYI *turns, his hand goes to his fly, he stops, turns round slowly.
A big grin appears on the faces of the other three.*)
What's the matter? No wan' pee-pee? Pee-pee pee-pee? No
more pee-pee? I know what it is.
(*Chanting.*)
Rem Acu . . .

OTHERS

Tetigisti, tetigisti . . .
(*As they go through the chant again* SI BERO *reappears with a
small bunch of herbs. They quickly stop singing.*)

CRIPPLE

Are we to come now, Si Bero? We need the work.

SI BERO

Wait here. I'll tell you when I'm ready.
(*They watch her pass. She goes into the* OLD WOMEN's *hut and*
AAFAA *sneaks near a moment later, to try and eavesdrop. The
others pass the time throwing dice. Action shifts to the* OLD
WOMEN's *hut.*)

IYA MATE

A-ah, you have a good eye, daughter.

IYA AGBA

Where did you find it?

SI BERO

Not far from where I went yesterday. Someone had emptied a
pile of rubbish near by, that's why I missed it.
(*The two* OLD WOMEN *move nearer the light, examining the
berries.*)

IYA MATE

The berries are all right too. Birds attack them quite early. You are lucky.

IYA AGBA

I wasn't expecting her to find any berries.

SI BERO (*dipping in the bag*)

I brought you some tobacco. And snuff for you, Iya Mate.

IYA MATE

You are a good woman. Some menfolk leave the home and never know whether they will come back to a dung heap or worse.

IYA AGBA

Weeds growing through the window and bats hanging from the rafters. That is when they find out that some women carry a curse in their breasts.

IYA MATE

Your menfolk are lucky. There will be leaves in their living room—but not the kind that places the handprint of death on a man's heart. Now, you leave these here.

IYA AGBA (*suddenly*)

Let me see that. Let me see it!

IYA MATE

What's the matter?

IYA AGBA

Bring it here. It's not the right one at all.

IYA MATE

Here. Look for yourself. No one can tell me my eyes are failing.

IYA AGBA

Just now I remember what you said—birds haven't attacked it. Usually it's the poison kind they don't go near.
(*She breaks the stalk.*)
I thought so. This is the twin. Poison.

19

SI BERO

Poison! But . . .

IYA MATE

It can't be poison.

IYA AGBA

They don't grow much. Haven't seen one in—oh, since I was a child. Farmers destroy them as soon as they see them. But it's the poison twin all right. Except for that red streak along the stalk you wouldn't tell them apart.

IYA MATE

I didn't even know there was the poison kind.

IYA AGBA

You don't see them much. Once in a lifetime. Farmers don't let them live, you know. Burn out the soil where they find it growing, just to kill the seeds. Foolishness. Poison has its uses too. You can cure with poison if you use it right. Or kill.

SI BERO

I'll throw it in the fire.

IYA MATE

Do nothing of the sort. You don't learn good things unless you learn evil.

SI BERO

But it's poison.

IYA MATE

It grows.

IYA AGBA

Rain falls on it.

IYA MATE

It sucks the dew.

IYA AGBA

It lives.

IYA MATE

It dies.

IYA AGBA

Same as any other. An-hn, same as any other.

SI BERO

That means I still have to find the right one.

IYA AGBA

It will be in the same place. They grow together most of the time.

SI BERO

I'll go tomorrow.

IYA MATE

Take some rest. Or . . . is he on his way home?

SI BERO

There is no news at all. I am beginning to . . .

IYA AGBA

Beginning to worry like every foolish woman. He'll come back. He and his father. There is too much binds them down here. They will take root with their spirit, not with their bodies on some unblessed soil. Let me see your hands.
(*She scrutinizes the hands carefully, bursts suddenly into a peal of laughter.*)
These hands are not yet ready to wind shrouds. We shall drink palm wine soon, very soon when someone returns.
(*She takes* SI BERO *by both hands and begins to shuffle with her, singing.*)
Ofe gbe wa de'le o—Ofe . . .
Ofe gbe wa de'le o—Ofe
Oko epo epa i runa
Gbe wa dele o
Ofe gbe wa d'le
(*The* MENDICANTS *look at one another, begin to beat time with*

*them, then join the singing in a raucous, cynical tone. The* WOMEN *stop, amazed and offended. The* OLD WOMEN *fold their arms, retire deeper into the hut while* SI BERO *dashes out, furious.*)

SI BERO

Stop that noise! Did I ask you here for entertainment?

CRIPPLE

No offence, Si Bero, no offence. We only thought you had forgotten us.

SI BERO

And thought your horrible voices the best way of reminding me.

GOYI

It's not our fault our voices are no better.

AAFAA

We can't all have voices like choiring angels, you know.

SI BERO

That's enough from you. Come along if you still want to work, only keep your voices down and stop frightening the neighbourhood.
(*They follow her to the front of the house.*)

CRIPPLE

So here we are, Si Bero. Bring out the herbs and let us catch the smell of something in your kitchen while we are about it.

AAFAA

How much are we getting today? Let's decide that first.

SI BERO

Depends how hard you work.

GOYI

Let's start work. It's a hot day and a man may as well stay close to shelter.

SI BERO

I have a whole sack my buyer brought in yesterday.

(*She takes hold of* BLINDMAN's *hand.*)
You can give me a hand, the sack is heavy.
(AAFAA *immediately positions himself to accompany her.*)
Not you, damn your forwardness. Did I talk to you?

AAFAA

He's not much use. He'll trip over and break his neck.

SI BERO

And that's his business not yours.
(*She leads* BLINDMAN *into the house.*)

AAFAA

Did you see that?

GOYI

I am sure even the Blindman did.

CRIPPLE

She didn't want any of us three, that was certain, but I . . .

AAFAA

Picks the one who can't see a thing.

CRIPPLE

I saw.

AAFAA

I told you it's funny business.

CRIPPLE

I am trying to tell you I saw. I saw the herbs.

AAFAA

Where? Where?

CRIPPLE

From here. From down here I could see through a gap in the door when she opened it.

AAFAA

What then? What did you see?

CRIPPLE

Herbs. Roots. Nothing but dried plants. The shelves are right up to the ceiling and they were full of leaves. All browned and crinkled.

GOYI

What kind?

CRIPPLE

All kinds.

GOYI

What is she going to do with all that forest?

AAFAA

Perhaps now you will learn to listen to me.

CRIPPLE

She must be slightly crazy. Living all alone, I suppose.

AAFAA

S-sh. They're coming. See if you can sneak another look.
(SI BERO *and* BLINDMAN *enter, carrying a heavy sack between them.*)

SI BERO

(*Entering backwards, she stumbles against the* CRIPPLE *who is trying to see through a crack.*)
Get out of the way, will you. Are you now the doorstop that I must step on you to get out of my own house?

CRIPPLE (*forced to retreat*)

You are in a bad mood today, Si Bero.

SI BERO

Your mother is in a bad mood, not me. Now get working instead of dragging yourself in people's way. Get busy. You know how I like them sorted out.

AAFAA

Yes, we know.

24

GOYI

First the roots.

CRIPPLE

Then peel the barks.

AAFAA

Slice the stalks.

CRIPPLE

Squeeze out the pulps.

GOYI

Pick the seeds.

AAFAA

Break the pods. Crack the plaster.

CRIPPLE

Probe the wound or it will never heal.

BLINDMAN

Cut off one root to save the other.

AAFAA

Cauterize.

CRIPPLE

Quick-quick-quick-quick, amputate!
(BLINDMAN *lets out a loud groan.*)

AAFAA

What do you mean, sir! How dare you lie there and whine?

GOYI

Cut his vocal cords.

AAFAA

"Before we operate we cut the vocal cords."

BLINDMAN

That's only for the dogs.

CRIPPLE

Your case is worse. You are an underdog.

GOYI

Rip out his vocal cords.
(BLINDMAN *lets out another scream.*)

AAFAA

We don't want you in this fraternity.

CRIPPLE

Fool! You should see the others and thank your stars.

BLINDMAN

I can't see them to thank.

AAFAA (*snatching his stick*)

Shall I put them on his head? He can have them in all colours.

CRIPPLE

Leave him for now, we'll simply expel him.

BLINDMAN (*screaming again*)

Oh God!

GOYI

Who's got the flaming sword?

AAFAA

Right here, Lord, right here.

GOYI

Show him the door.

AAFAA

Out of the garden, bum, don't ever show your face in here again.

BLINDMAN

I appeal.

CRIPPLE

Who to?

BLINDMAN

As.

AAFAA

In the name of As of the beginning, out!

BLINDMAN

No!

AAFAA

Out!

BLINDMAN

No!

AAFAA

One—Two—Three—Four—

BLINDMAN (*druggedly*)

Five—Six—Seven—Eight—Nine—

AAFAA

Out!

BLINDMAN (*wearily*)

Out!

(*His head drops down.* AAFAA *raises the "sword."*)

SI BERO

Have you all gone mad?

AAFAA

No. I'm quite good at it, actually. One stroke and—clean through the tendons. Bang through the ball-and-socket, believe me. I never touch the marrow.

GOYI

Heh, stop. The woman.

SI BERO

I said have you gone mad? Are you here to work or fool around?

CRIPPLE

Oh, never mind us. Come on.

(*They settle down quickly. As the sack is emptied on the ground,* si bero, *already about to turn into the house, stops, goes over and picks out a bunch of roots which she turns about in her hand, inspecting it. The* mendicants *cannot contain their curiosity, directly observing her action.* blindman *listens intensely into the silence. Finally she starts towards the* old women's *hut.*)

AAFAA

We can sort that bunch if you like. And give it a scraping. It seems dirty enough.

si bero (*turns slowly on him*)

Not half as dirty as your anus. The day you scrape that you can tell me what needs scraping and what doesn't.

AAFAA (*raising his stick*)

You go too far with that mouth of yours!

(si bero *looks him up and down contemptuously. She continues on her way.*)

I have a mind to set fire to every single herb in that house.

BLINDMAN

Why don't you learn to leave her alone?

AAFAA

What did I do? What did I say? Just because of one stinking root. She has a mouth like a running gutter.

BLINDMAN

Leave the woman alone. She minds her own business, you mind yours.

AAFAA

And that's enough from you, Mr. Blind Advocate. I don't have to listen to you take her side all the time. One more word from you . . .

28

(*He feints a slap across* BLINDMAN's *face.* BLINDMAN, *alert, springs suddenly backwards and grasps his staff.* AAFAA *looks at him a moment, then bursts out laughing.*)

Do you see what I see? The man actually wants to fight me. Did you see? Did you see him? He has no eyes but he actually wants to fight. Hm? Is it really a fight you're looking for, Blind One? (*He kicks aside his staff, but* BLINDMAN *immediately closes in on* AAFAA, *reaches for his arms and imprisons them. They strain against each other.*)

CRIPPLE

Bloody fools!

GOYI

Look! The specialist.
(*He points to the spot where they were first seen. Standing there is* BERO, *uniformed, carrying a briefcase. He watches. The* CRIPPLE *tugs at the clothes of the struggling men.*)

CRIPPLE

Better stop that, he's here.

GOYI

He's waiting for us. Come on.
(*The two men break apart.* AAFAA *is panting heavily. The* CRIPPLE *dashes quickly and brings* BLINDMAN *his stick. Somewhat sheepishly they troop towards* BERO.)

BERO (*giving them a long cold stare*)

Was that what I sent you to do in that house?

AAFAA

He started it. And the woman.

CRIPPLE

Aafaa hit him first. Knocked off his stick. A blind man too.
(*He spits.*)

29

AAFAA

If people know they have a handicap then they shouldn't open their mouths to provoke their betters.

CRIPPLE

Hits a blind man.
(*He spits again.*)

AAFAA

If you think just because you are a cripple you won't get it from me if you go beyond bounds, just try it and see.

CRIPPLE

A blind man.
(*He spits again.*)

AAFAA (*raising the rattle threateningly*)

Don't think because of him being here I can't . . .
(*The* CRIPPLE *counters immediately by raising his crutch.*)

BERO

Shut up! Shut up all of you. I didn't send you to the house to fight. I asked you to keep your eyes open and keep her from going down.
(*He looks at them with contempt, then jerks his thumb in the direction of the cellar.*)
What about him. Is he staying quiet?

AAFAA (*jerking his thumb at* BLINDMAN)

Ask him. He is the only one who got to enter the house. Ask Blindman what he saw.

BERO

I have no time for fooling.

BLINDMAN

He was quiet. I don't think the woman knows anything.

BERO

What room did you enter?

30

**BLINDMAN**

The one with the herbs. I don't think there are any bare walls in there; it's all covered with herbs. From the floor to the ceiling, it's all full of herbs very carefully laid and touched and dusted every day of her life. I could tell that as soon as I entered.

**CRIPPLE**

I saw it. I caught a glimpse.

**AAFAA**

Last night when we got him into that underground place she was fast asleep. We didn't make a noise.

**BLINDMAN**

Excuse me, I wish to say something.

**BERO**

Yes?

**BLINDMAN**

I can only tell you what I felt—in that room where I stood with her. There is more love in there than you'll find in the arms of a hundred women. I don't know what unhappiness you intend for her but . . .

**BERO**

That's enough. You don't know a thing about anything, so shut up.

(BLINDMAN *shrugs and retires to one side.*)

**GOYI**

My feeling is, I can't help agreeing with him. In any case we are not much use to anyone.

**BERO**

I said that's enough. You're under orders.

**AAFAA**

I am not. And I haven't eaten today.

BERO

Very good.

AAFAA

Enh? Say that again. Which of what is very good?

BERO

The fact that you haven't eaten today. If you fall down on the job you know you will go back to being hungry.

AAFAA

Good. I am glad to hear where we stand. We've done one thing already and don't think it was easy getting him in that hole without waking the neighbours or your sister. So what about for now? Have we already fallen down on the job that we see nothing of what you promised?

BERO

(*He studies him for a while, then turns to the others.*)
Have you told him who I am exactly?

AAFAA

Oh yes, Dr. Bero. I know who you are. The specialist. We all do. So what about it? You say we are under orders but I tell you I am not. I know these three are discharged. As for me, I have never even taken orders from you before.

BERO

These are no longer discharged and you now take orders from me. You either get that into your twisted mind or get out now.

AAFAA

You can't tell me to get out. We teamed together without your help and we are not doing badly as it is. You can't come here and break us up. If we have anybody to thank it's him down there. Not that I care. I always thought he was crazy. But just don't you forget we are a team—one for all and all for one.

BERO

You prefer that? Begging for pennies and getting spat upon?

AAFAA

That's what you think. Ho ho, that's a good one, isn't it? Isn't it? You don't know anything about us, do you? Think we spent all that time with your old man without learning a thing or two? You can't specialize in everything, you know.

GOYI

Shut up, Aafaa.

CRIPPLE

You talk too much, shut your mouth.

BERO

He's saying nothing I don't know already.

AAFAA

You know nothing, Dr. Bero. You can't bluff me.

BLINDMAN

You really are a fool, Aafaa.

CRIPPLE (*whining*)

Pay no attention to him. We do nothing really bad, just one or two things to eke out the droppings of charity.

BERO

Save that for your customers. I'm not interested in what you've done. But from now on you stop taking any risks. I don't want to have to look for you in every filthy gaol.

CRIPPLE

If you'll make up for our losses, sir . . . we were on our way to greater things.

GOYI

I'll say that for us. We were just beginning.

BERO

To do what?

CRIPPLE

Well, you know . . . your Old Man did come up with some ripe ideas . . .

BERO

You'll be taken care of. That's a promise.

CRIPPLE

Then as I said before, that's all right by me.

GOYI

Me too.

AAFAA

No, it isn't. I don't mind the risks we are taking right now . . .

BERO

I said, no more risks.

AAFAA

That's for us to decide until you say how much. What does he know about risks anyway? Even if I was only a chaplain to the men out there I knew what risk was. I nearly had it once or twice. Quite different from working for Intelligence where all you had to do was sift through papers full of lies and know how to slap people around . . .

(BERO *cuts him across the face with his swagger stick.* AAFAA *staggers back, clutching the wound.* BERO *stands still, watching him. At the sound of pain* IYA AGBA *looks out of the hut and impassively observes the scene.*)

BERO

That should remind you I do know how to slap people around. And you'd better remember some other things I know. You weren't just discharged because of your—sickness. Just remember that . . . and other things.

*(He stands gazing towards the house for a while.)*
I am due home now. You know when to follow. Just remember
to carry out my instructions to the letter.
*(He walks purposefully to the house. As he passes by the* OLD
WOMEN's *hut,* IYA AGBA *leans back to avoid being seen by him. A
moment later* SI BERO *emerges, sees* BERO *and shouts, running
towards him.* IYA MATE *joins the other women to watch the
reunion.)*

SI BERO

Bero! Bero!
*(She embraces him, then tears herself off and shouts.)*

BERO

Don't do that!

SI BERO

*(Rushing about, she doesn't hear.)*
He's home! He's . . .

BERO

*(He chases after and restrains her.)*
Be quiet!

SI BERO

What?

BERO

I don't want my return announced.

SI BERO

Why not?
*(Suddenly suspicious.)*
You're not going back again, are you?

BERO

It isn't that. I want some quiet, that's all.

SI BERO

Oh! how thoughtless I was. But they will be disappointed.

35

BERO

Who will?

SI BERO

Our neighbours. All your old patients.

BERO

Corpses.

SI BERO

What? I said your old patients.

BERO

I said corpses. Oh, forget it.

SI BERO

I can't.
(*She scans his face anxiously.*)
They haven't forgotten you.

BERO

They still exist, do they?

SI BERO (*again puzzled*)

Who? I don't understand.

BERO

I'm tired. Let's talk of something else.

SI BERO

Oh yes, you must be. Come inside. No, wait. You mustn't come in yet. Be patient now, Bero. (*She hurries into the house.*) Don't move from there. Stand still.
(BERO *looks slowly round him, he gazes as if he is trying to pierce through walls into neighbouring homes. The expression on his face is contempt.*

SI BERO *reappears with a gourd of palm wine, pours it on the ground in front of the doorstep. Then she moves to unlace his boots.*)

BERO

You still keep up these little habits.

SI BERO

I like to keep close to earth.

BERO

(*He steps back to prevent her from taking off his boots.*)
Bare feet, wet earth. We've wetted your good earth with something more potent than that, you know.

SI BERO

Not you. Neither you nor Father. You had nothing to do with it. On the contrary.

BERO

What, on the contrary?

SI BERO

Were you together? Did you manage to work together?

BERO

We were together. For some time.

SI BERO

Is he going to stay with us?

BERO

We'll . . . discuss him later.

SI BERO (*suddenly fearful*)

What is it, Bero? Is he . . . ?

BERO

(*He stares back at her, letting the pause hang.*)
Well, is he—what?

SI BERO (*laughing*)

Stop trying to frighten me.

BERO

Who's trying to?

37

SI BERO

Where are you hiding him? I bet he's waiting round the corner.

BERO

He'll rejoin us in his own time.

SI BERO (*disappointed*)

Oh. But he's safe.

BERO (*impatiently*)

Of course he is.

SI BERO (*taking his hand*)

Come with me. I must show you to the Old Women and tell them also Father is safe.

BERO

What Old Women?

SI BERO

Over there in the hut.

BERO

Who are they?

SI BERO

Herbalists. They helped me with your work.

BERO

But why bring them here? Why camp them on my doorstep?

SI BERO

They were good to me. I couldn't have done a thing without them. Come and talk to them.

(BERO *does not move. Immediately, the* OLD WOMEN *start to speak.* BERO *and* SI BERO *remain still,* BERO *looking towards the* OLD WOMEN'S *hut while* SI BERO *watches him.*)

IYA AGBA

Well, has it been worth it, do you think?

IYA MATE

It's good to see her face bubbling like froth on good wine.

IYA AGBA

Not her, him!

IYA MATE

Oh, him. Well, you never can tell with seeds. The plant may be good . . . but we'll know, we'll know.

IYA AGBA

I hope it's a good seed. That was two lives we poured into her hands. Two long lives spent pecking at secrets grain by grain.

IYA MATE

More than two. What she took from us began with others we no longer call by name.

IYA AGBA

She sucked my head dry.

IYA MATE

She is a good woman.

IYA AGBA

Yes, but what about him?

IYA MATE

You sense something wrong in him?

IYA AGBA

It's my life that's gone into his. I haven't burrowed so deep to cast good earth on worthless seeds.

IYA MATE

Nor she. Tramping through all those bushes, finding the desolate spots only we remember.

IYA AGBA

She was stubborn, others would have given up early.
(*She giggles.*)

I did my best to put her off. Sent her on those fruitless errands, hoping she'd give up. Others would have done.

IYA MATE

Oh, you are wicked.

IYA AGBA

She proved herself, there's no denying it. She proved herself. If she'd wanted it easy or simply out of greed I would have guided her feet into quicksands and left her there.

IYA MATE

You would, I know you, you would.

IYA AGBA

So let him watch it. I haven't come this far to put my whole being in a sieve.

(*She turns abruptly and returns into the hut.* IYA MATE *remains for a while.*)


SI BERO

They told me what to look for, where to look for it. How to sort them and preserve them.

BERO (*nods*)

You haven't wasted your time. I still need things from my former vocation.

SI BERO

Former vocation?

BERO

A means, not an end.

SI BERO

We heard terrible things. So much evil. Then I would console myself that I earned the balance by carrying on your work. One thing cancels out another. Bero, they're waiting. Go and greet them, Bero. They held your life together while you were away.

BERO

What is that supposed to mean?

SI BERO

I never feared for you while they were here.

BERO

You really disappoint me. You are supposed to be intelligent. It was you I asked to do my work, not some stupid old hags. I suppose they filled your hand with all that evil stuff. You've been pretty free with that word.

SI BERO

Not you yourself, Bero, but guilt contaminates. And often I was afraid . . .
(*Suddenly determined.*)
Bero, where is Father!?

BERO

Safe.

SI BERO (*stubbornly*)

But you must know when he's coming.

BERO

Sometime.

SI BERO

When? Why didn't you return together?

BERO

He's a sick man. He is coming home to be cured.

SI BERO

Sick? Wounded?

BERO

Mind sickness. We must be kind to him.

SI BERO

How long, Bero? How long had he been sick?

41

BERO

Ever since he came out. Maybe the . . . suffering around him proved too much for him. His mind broke under the strain.

SI BERO (*quietly*)

How bad? Don't hide anything, Bero. How bad is he?

BERO

He started well. But of course we didn't know which way his mind was working. Madmen have such diabolical cunning. It was fortunate I had already proved myself. He was dangerous. Dangerous!

SI BERO

What do you mean? Did he endanger you?

BERO

Did he! He was in a different sector, working among the convalescents. I wouldn't have known what was going on if I had still been with the Medical Corps.

SI BERO

If you had still been?

BERO

I told you. I switched.

SI BERO

But how? You have your training. How does one switch, just like that?

BERO

You are everything once you go out there. In an emergency . . . (*He shrugs.*)
The head of the Intelligence Section died rather suddenly. Natural causes.

SI BERO

And that's the new vocation?

BERO

None other, sister, none other. The Big Braids agreed I was born into it. Not that that was any recommendation. They are all submental apes.

SI BERO

(*She studies him avidly, a slow apprehension beginning to show on her face.*)
But you have . . . you have given that up now. You are back to your real work. Your practice.

BERO (*turning calmly to meet her gaze*)
Practice? Yes, I intend to maintain that side of my practice. A laboratory is important. Everything helps. Control, sister, control. Power comes from bending Nature to your will. The Specialist they called me, and a specialist is—well—a specialist. You analyse, you diagnose, you—
(*He aims an imaginary gun.*)
—prescribe.

SI BERO (*more to herself*)
You should have told me. I have made pledges I cannot fulfil.

BERO

Pledges? What are you talking about?

SI BERO

I swore I was sure of you, only then would they help me.

BERO

Who? The Old Women?

SI BERO

They held nothing back from me.
(*The* PRIEST *enters, hails them from a distance.*)

PRIEST

A-ah, there you are. Bero, my boy, welcome home. I caught a glimpse of you from my vestry and I said, No, it's not him, it

43

can't be. But of course, who else could it be looking so handsome and imposing. Your prayers are answered, I said to myself, your prayers are answered, you Doubting Thomas. And how is the little lady, the courageous one who kept the fort in the absence of brother and father? Overjoyed, I am sure, overjoyed. So are we all.

(*He observes nothing of* BERO's *cold attitude nor the fact that* BERO *has moved casually away from the patronizing arm which he tried to place on his shoulder.*)

I meant to call on one or two neighbours on the way but that's just the selfish sinner I am, may God forgive me. No, I decided, I'll just have him all to myself for a little bit.

BERO

That's rather lucky.

PRIEST

Beg your pardon?

SI BERO

He's tired, Pastor. Don't let it out he's back yet.

PRIEST

Of course not. I wouldn't dream of doing such a thing. We all have our human failings of course, but I do know how inconsiderate people can be in their joys. Wouldn't think a man who's just returned from the seventh outpost of hell would want a little time to himself. I've suffered from my old complaint, you know, my boy, but I can suffer a little longer. Just get settled, son, just get settled and give yourself a well-deserved rest.

SI BERO

Pastor, you know I offered you . . .

PRIEST

Not quite the same thing, young lady, not quite the same thing. The doctor used to make those extracts with his own hand and . . .

SI BERO

It was the same one he made before he left.

PRIEST

No no, I could tell the difference. Oh yes, I could tell.

SI BERO

It was the same.

PRIEST

Good of you to try, but no. You just didn't make it the same.
I could tell the difference at once. As soon as you're rested, my
boy, as soon as you've rested . . . oh dear me. How shameful.
Here I am complaining of my little fits and I haven't even asked
news of my good friend. When is your father coming, my lad?

BERO

Soon.

SI BERO

Bero was just telling me . . .

PRIEST

Soon. How soon?

BERO

Soon enough.

PRIEST

Not soon enough for me, boy, not soon enough. I can't wait to
take issue with him on all our old debates. Such an argumentative man, your father, such an argumentative man. And he'll
have some stories to tell me, I'm sure. Really looking forward to
our long evenings together. What an experience he must have
had, what an experience! You know, it's strange how these dis-
asters bring out the very best in man—and the worst sometimes.
In your father's case, of course, the very best. Truly noble. I
couldn't believe my ears when he got up one day and said he
was going to join you. At your age, I said, you doddering old

thing? I used to call him that, you know, and he would call me
the mitred hypocrite. All in play, of course, only in play. So he
. . . where was I? Something about your father, I believe. Oh
yes, he suddenly got up one evening, right in the midst of our
argument and said, I am going to see what's going on. He was
just reading me a letter from you and he got all worked up. It
can't be, he shouted. And then he leapt up and said—right out
of the blue—we've got to legalize cannibalism. Yes, right out
of the blue. What do you mean, I said, thinking he only wanted
to start another argument. But no, he repeats it over and over
and of course, I took him on. Legalize cannibalism? It's a damnable and heathenish idea. Yes, that's how we started the argument. Warmest session we ever had together. He wouldn't
yield one foot and I wouldn't budge one inch. Not one fraction
of an inch. My polemical spirit was aroused. Not to talk of
Christian principles. For three hours I fought him foot by foot.
Never been in better form. Nearly all night we argued, if you
please, and then in the morning he was gone. What do you make
of that?

SI BERO

Pastor, I think Bero is a little tired . . .

PRIEST

Had only one letter from him all that time. Told me he was
doing recuperative work among some disabled fellows. No for-
warding address, if you please. I couldn't even continue our old
debate by post. Strange man, your father, very strange. You
didn't run into him out there, did you? I'm really anxious to
know if he still intends to legalize cannibalism.

BERO

He does.

PRIEST

I knew it. A stubborn man, once he gets hold of an idea. You
won't believe it but he actually said to me, I'm going to try and

persuade those fools not to waste all that meat. Mind you he never could stand wastage, could he? I remember he used to wade into you both if he caught you wasting anything. But human flesh, why, that's another matter altogether.

BERO

But why, Pastor. It's quite delicious, you know.

PRIEST

Just what I say. It's . . . what did you say?

BERO

(*He reaches out and pulls out the* PRIEST'*s cheek.*)
This. Delicious.

PRIEST (*struggling free*)

You're joking, of course.

BERO

No. Your friend will confirm it when he comes.

PRIEST (*increasingly horrified*)

You mean he . . .

BERO

No, not him. He never meant anything. At least, not that way. But we found it delicious just the same.

PRIEST

You?

BERO

I give you the personal word of a scientist. Human flesh is delicious. Of course, not all parts of the body. I prefer the balls myself.

PRIEST (*vehemently*)

I don't believe you.

BERO

You don't? Well, then, why don't you stay to dinner?

PRIEST

Dinner?

(*Cheering up.*)

Of course. I see all you want is an argument like your old man. Delighted, of course. Only too delighted to oblige . . .

(*He is stricken by a sudden doubt.*)

Er . . . dinner . . . did you say dinner?

BERO

Dinner. I came well-laden with supplies.

(*The* PRIEST *glances at* BERO'S *bulging briefcase lying near by, gulps.*)

PRIEST

I . . . er . . . I am wondering if I haven't got a little christening to attend to. I . . . er . . . couldn't simply come for drinks afterwards?

BERO

A christening so late in the evening?

PRIEST

Well, you know, the blessing at home and all that. The christening was this morning.

(*He is already retreating.*)

God bless you, my children both. I shall hurry back as soon as it's all over. Can't get rid of these extra parish duties . . . welcome back once again, my boy . . .

(*They watch him take flight.*)

SI BERO (*laughing*)

You know, for a moment I nearly believed you.

BERO

Oh?

(*He turns and looks at her pityingly.*)

You didn't?

(*Pause. They look each other in the face. Her laughter dies slowly.*)

SI BERO

Oh God.

BERO

Out of your world, little sister, out of your little world. Stay in it and do only what I tell you. That way you'll be safe.

SI BERO (*vehemently*)

Abomination!

BERO

Delicious, you heard me say.

SI BERO

Abomination!

BERO (*with deliberate cruelty*)

Delicious. The balls, to be exact. I thought I told you to stay in your little world! Go and take tea with the senile pastor or gossip with your old women. Don't come out from where you're safe.
(*Quietly.*)
Or sane.

SI BERO

But at least tell me why? In God's name why?

BERO

No, not in God's name—in the name of As!

SI BERO

What?

BERO

As. The new god and the old—As.

SI BERO

What are you trying to be, Bero—evil?

49

BERO

Does it sound that bad? It was no brainchild of mine. We thought it was a joke. I'll bless the meat, he said. And then— As Was the Beginning, As is, Now, As Ever shall be . . . world without. . . . We said amen with a straight face and sat down to eat. Then, afterwards . . .

SI BERO

Yes?

BERO

He told us.
(*Pause. He laughs suddenly.*)
But why not? Afterwards I said, why not? What is one flesh from another? So I tried it again, just to be sure of myself. It was the first step to power you understand. Power in its purest sense. The end of inhibitions. The conquest of the weakness of your too-human flesh with all its sentiment. So again, all to my-self I said Amen to his grace.

SI BERO

I don't follow you, Bero. Who said grace? Whose words are these?

BERO

Father's part of the liturgy of his bedridden audience. Wait a minute.
(*He points to the* MENDICANTS.)
They can tell you more about it.

SI BERO

Who? These? What they have to do with . . . ?

BERO

Have you never thought how they came to beg so close to here? At the beginning, that is. Before I found out about them.

SI BERO

Oh, is that it? You mean he sent them? But you know him—
Liberty House. It's not a crime. I found them work to do.

BERO (*heatedly*)

It's not his charitable propensities I am concerned with. Father's
assignment was to help the wounded readjust to the pieces and
remnants of their bodies. Physically. Teach them to make bas-
kets if they still had fingers. To use their mouths to ply needles
if they had none, or use it to sing if their vocal cords had not
been shot away. Teach them to amuse themselves, make something of themselves. Instead he began to teach them to think,
think, THINK! Can you picture a more treacherous deed than
to place a working mind in a mangled body?

SI BERO

Where is he?

BERO

Where? Here.

SI BERO

Here?

BERO (*pointing to the* MENDICANTS)

There. When they open their mouths you can hear him. You!
Come here! Tell her. Would you call yourself sane?
(*The* MENDICANTS *have approached,* AAFAA *in the lead.*)

AAFAA

Certainly not, sir.

BERO

You got off lightly. Why?

AAFAA

I pleaded insanity.

BERO

Who made you insane?

AAFAA (*by rote, raising his eyes to heaven*)

The Old Man, sir. He said things, he said things. My mind . . . I beg your pardon, sir, the thing I call my mind, well, was no longer there. He took advantage of me, sir, in that convalescent home. I was unconscious long stretches at a time. Whatever I saw when I came to was real. Whatever voice I heard was the truth. It was always him. Bending over my bed. I asked him, Who are you? He answered, The one and only truth.

CRIPPLE

Hear hear.

GOYI

Same here.

AAFAA

Always at me, he was, sir. I plead insanity.

CRIPPLE

Hear hear.

GOYI

Same here.

AAFAA (*pointing to* BLINDMAN)

Even him.

BLINDMAN

Once I even thought I could see him.

GOYI

Oh, but you did, you did.

BLINDMAN

No, not really.

CRIPPLE

You did, you did. The picture forms in the mind, remember?

52

GOYI

His very words. But any fool knows they form on the eye.

AAFAA

Lord, he mixed us up.

BLINDMAN

You can see me, he said, you can see me. Look at me with your mind. I swear I began to see him. Then I knew I was insane.

CRIPPLE

Hear hear.

GOYI

Same here.

AAFAA

We all did.

CRIPPLE

And getting me all choosy!

BLINDMAN

Poor you.

CRIPPLE

Beggars can't be choosers, we all knew that.

AAFAA

Yet he got you choosy.

CRIPPLE

I was mad.

BLINDMAN (*changing his voice*)

Remember, even if you have nothing left but your vermin, discriminate between one bug and the next.

CRIPPLE

Some bugs are friendly, others wild.

GOYI

The one sucks gently, the other nips.

53

BLINDMAN

If you must eat a toad . . .

CRIPPLE

. . . pick the fat one, with eggs in its belly.

AAFAA

Listen to the fool. It's you he's calling a toad.
(*The* CRIPPLE *advances on him.*)

GOYI

No, it wasn't. Don't listen to him.

AAFAA (*voice change*)

You'll listen now or you'll listen later!

SI BERO

Where is Father?

AAFAA

Where is he, where is he? As is everywhere.

CRIPPLE (*picking a flea from his rags*)

Got him!

SI BERO (*turning sharply*)

What!

CRIPPLE (*throwing it in his mouth*)

A fat one.

GOYI

Greedy beggar.

AAFAA

Did you choose it?

CRIPPLE

It chose me.

BLINDMAN

Chose? An enemy of As.

**AAFAA**

Sure? Not a disciple.

**BLINDMAN**

An enemy. Subversive agent.

**AAFAA**

Quite right. As chooses, man accepts. Had it sucked any blood?

**CRIPPLE**

It tasted bloody.

**GOYI**

Accept my sympathies.

**CRIPPLE**

Not needed. The blood is back where it belongs.

**AAFAA**

The cycle is complete?

**CRIPPLE**

Definitely.

**GOYI**

Then you can't complain.

**SI BERO**

What is this, Bero? Where is Father?

**AAFAA**

Within the cycle.

**BLINDMAN**

That's good. The **cycle of As.** Tell the Old Man that—he'll be pleased.

**SI BERO**

Where is he?

**AAFAA**

Where the cycle is complete there will As be found. As of the beginning, we praise thee.

SI BERO (*shutting her ears*)

Oh God!

BERO (*pointing to the* MENDICANTS)

Do you still want to see him?

AAFAA

As—Was—Is—Now.

SI BERO

Shut up, you loathsome toads!
(*There is a brief silence. They all look at her.*)

AAFAA (*grinning*)

Toads again. You hear that?

CRIPPLE

She was looking at you.

AAFAA

What! I must say I feel insulted.

CRIPPLE

A man must have some pride.

GOYI

My pride is—As.

AAFAA

And all in the line of duty. Sir, I demand protection.

BERO

That's enough. Open the surgery.
(*He turns to* SI BERO.)
You want to see him? You shall.

MENDICANTS (*already moving towards the clinic*)

As—Was—Is—Now—As Ever Shall Be . . .
Bi o ti wa
Ni yio se wa
Bi o ti wa

Ni yio se wa
Bi o ti wa l'atete ko se . . .

SI BERO

And what in God's name is that?

BERO

One of their chants.
(*He grabs her arm as she tries to run after the* MENDICANTS.)
Now listen, and always remember this—he is wholly in my
charge.

SI BERO

How long? How long has he been home?

BERO

Home? What home? I tell you he is here in my charge. It was
either this or . . . Do not interfere!
(*He holds her with his eyes for a few moments, then moves to
follow the* MENDICANTS. *He stops when he sees that she has made
no attempt to follow.*)
You want to see him? Come on.
(*Pause.* SI BERO *looks at him with increasing horror and disbelief.
She turns and runs towards the* OLD WOMEN *who receive her at
the door of the hut.* BERO *goes on into the clinic where the light
has come on, revealing the* OLD MAN *seated in the midst of the
chanting* MENDICANTS. *Lights fade slowly.*)

# Part Two

*(The clinic, below the ground floor of the house. An examination couch, assortment of a few instruments and jars in a locked glass case, a chromium sterilizing unit, etc., a table, swivel chair etc. A white smock hangs against a shelf, with surgical mask and gloves tucked in the pockets. The* MENDICANTS *are crouched, standing, stooping in their normal postures, humming their chant and listlessly throwing dice. The* OLD MAN's *attitude varies from boredom to tolerant amusement.)*

AAFAA

A. As is Acceptance, Adjustment. Adjustment of Ego to the Acceptance of As . . . hm. Not bad. B . . . B. . . .
*(His eye roams over the room for inspiration, falls on the* BLIND-MAN.)
Of course. B, Blindness. Blindness in As. I say this unto you, As is all-seeing; All shall see in As who render themselves blind to all else. C . . . C?
*(He looks at the others one by one but ends up shaking his head.)*
No, nothing from you lot this time. Can't see how I can ask the flock to get crippled for some reward in As. C . . . No, I'll have to skip it for now. D—good—I don't have to go far for that. D, Divinity. That's us. For Destiny too. In fact Destiny first, then Divinity. Destiny is the Duty of Divinity. D-D-D—Destiny in 3-Dimension. We the Divinity shall guide the flock along the path of Destiny. E . . .

BLINDMAN

Epilepsy?

AAFAA *(sharply)*

Watch your mouth!

BLINDMAN

For your Divinity to have control, the flock must be without control. Epilepsy seems to be the commonest form—at least, I have witnessed much that is similar.

GOYI

I know what you mean. Taken by the spirit, they call it. It's a good circus turn any day. Aafaa should know.

AAFAA

You are not suggesting I exploited human infirmities, are you?

CRIPPLE

I wish I had the power. Gives a man a sense of power to watch others twitch like so many broken worms. Broken worms, ah, that's a fine thing to come from my mouth.

AAFAA

Before we get to Z, I promise you your private and personal consolation. F ... F ... F ...

GOYI

As Farts, damn you!
(*He turns his rear and gestures obscenely.*)

AAFAA

I was going to suggest Fulfils. As fulfils.

GOYI

And I say Farts.

AAFAA

Are you going to confront your Destiny with a fart?

GOYI

I have done before. I did it in that place where they treated us. Treatment! No doctor. Only nurses who couldn't tell a man's end from their own. Hey, listen, and let me tell you, it was the cleverest thing I ever thought all those sweet times we spent with the Old Man. With him saying this and saying that to us and me on my side—couldn't turn on my back and couldn't turn on my belly—and the sun would come up one day and I wouldn't see it again until it come up the next. One time he told us—remember that day?—he told us the earth goes round and round, which if you remember was just too much for someone like me to swallow. So, the following morning when the sun came round again, I said to myself, well, I suppose the Old Man must be right. I don't know what makes the world go round but I do know what goes round the world. It's wind. And I broke it loudly and felt better.

CRIPPLE

Dirty pig.

GOYI

It's all very well for you to talk. You could get around even then. I sometimes think God made you out of rubber or something.

AAFAA

(*He has been thinking his own thoughts, gives a sudden shout.*) God, that's it. Godhead! What a real pagan I've become if that took me so long. G, As is Godhead. I is next.

BLINDMAN

I am I, what more do you want?

AAFAA (*chews it over*)

I am I, thus sayeth As. No . . . that might cause trouble.

BLINDMAN

What kind of trouble?

AAFAA

Think of yourself. Sooner or later someone is going to say it and leave out "so sayeth As." And that means trouble.

GOYI

I don't follow.

63

CRIPPLE

Ask the Old Man. He'll settle the question.
(*They turn towards the* OLD MAN, *but he is still motionless, unresponsive.*)

AAFAA

Old Man, what do you think of the I matter?
(*Again they wait in vain for his response.*)
All right, if that doesn't interest you, at least give us something between I and Z. That is still a long way to go and already I can feel my brain giving out. Not to talk of the others. Anything you like, your forgotten wishes, your deepest cravings, your pet dreams . . .

GOYI

S-sh!

CRIPPLE

Why do you keep making fun of him? Leave him alone.

AAFAA

(*He looks genuinely surprised.*)
But I . . .

GOYI

That's what he used to say. You were using his very words just to mock him.

AAFAA

Well, I didn't mean to.
(*His apparent contrition leaves the others a little flat. They steal furtive glances at the* OLD MAN, *who does not move.*)

CRIPPLE

I have a pet dream.

AAFAA

We know what that is, so shut up!

64

BLINDMAN

I want to hear his pet dream.

AAFAA

Can't you guess what it is by seeing where he scratches himself at night?

BLINDMAN

No, I cannot see.
(*A brief pause.*)

CRIPPLE

I'll tell you. Every night we sleep in this place I have that same dream. It's what makes me stay on. It is what makes me . . . assist . . .

AAFAA

Collaborate.

CRIPPLE

I don't know what the big word means.

BLINDMAN (*gently*)

No. Don't bother with it. Continue with your dream.

CRIPPLE

It is what makes me continue to obey the specialist.
(*Pause.*)

OLD MAN

(*Unnoticed, he has turned round to face them.*)
Go on, your dream.

CRIPPLE

(*For a moment he, with the rest, shows confusion.*)
I . . . dream he tells me to get on that table. He says, I could not attend to you before but there were other things . . . one thing at a time, certain things are more important than others. So he operates on my back and in another moment he's finished, wipes his hands and says . . .

65

AAFAA

Arise, throw off thy crutches and follow me.

CRIPPLE

(*He lowers his eyes as if in abashment.*)
Yes, more or less the same words. But just as I want to get up, I
wake up from the blasted dream!

AAFAA (*with explosive disgust*)

That's a permanent dream if ever I heard one. You think the
specialist has time for your petty little inconvenience? You're
getting to be quite important in your mind to afford dreams
like that. I wouldn't dare. Would you?
(*He turns to* GOYI. *The* CRIPPLE *turns his head in confusion.*)
Oh, you too? What have we here? A conspiracy of the élite?
I suppose you too have been dreaming you'll get back your
sight from him? No, I should have known you better. Just these
two.
(*Explosively.*)
You are just the kind of people who make life impossible for
professionals. Miracle, Miracle! That's all we ever get out of
your smelly mouths. Because you blackmailed one Christ into
showing off once in a while you think all others are suckers for
that kind of showmanship. Well, you've met your match this
generation. Turn left, turn right, turn right about again, you'll
find everyone you meet is more than a match for you.
(*A short pause.*)

BLINDMAN

Isn't it time for his food?

AAFAA

The little woman will knock when it's ready. And let him
starve a bit anyway, why not? He got us into this mess. If there
is one thing I can't stand it's amateurs. Even there I didn't like
him all that much. Now the specialist—that's a professional. You
only need to remember it's father and son. Human beings both

66

of them. Who is my neighbour, you know—all that stuff and
sentiment.

(*A knock on the door. They all fall silent. The three seeing*
MENDICANTS *dart a look at the* OLD MAN. *The knock is repeated.*)
All right, we heard. Put down the tray and go back to your hole.
Go on. Get going.

(*They listen to the footsteps retreat out of hearing.* AAFAA *chants
at the* OLD MAN.)
Lord, now lettest thou thy servant depart in peace, according
to thy word.

(*To* BLINDMAN.)
Are you going to open the door?

(BLINDMAN *sighs, gets up, followed by* GOYI. *He unbolts the
door and* GOYI *exits. He bolts it again,* AAFAA *watching every
movement.*)
Chop time, Old Man. Your food is on the way.

OLD MAN

Did you take my watch?

(*He stirs and feels in his breast pocket.*)

AAFAA

It was broken. I sent it for repairs.

OLD MAN

You have it on your wrist.

AAFAA

Mistaken identity.

(*He holds up his wrist.*)
Take a look if you like.

OLD MAN

You took my glasses also.

AAFAA (*dips into his pocket*)

Try these. No? They might just fit you never can tell. They
used to belong to him.

67

(*He points to* BLINDMAN.)
Are you sure you wouldn't try them? After the blast took off his eyes—that's how we first met—it was my job to go round comforting the poor fools—or burying them. Anyway—and that's the strange thing; the glasses were knocked off all right, but not a scratch on them. So he says, take my glasses from that bedside cupboard in case someone else needs them. I've kept them ever since. Are you sure you won't try them?

OLD MAN

Let me see that watch again.

AAFAA

It won't tell you anything.

OLD MAN

Which of you took my glasses?

AAFAA

What does it matter?

OLD MAN

I want to see what's in the food. What are you giving me to eat?

AAFAA

Leave that to us.
(*A sudden peremptory knock on the door. Enter* BERO, *followed by* GOYI *bearing a tray of food.*)

BERO

I thought I would join you for dinner.

OLD MAN (*rounding on him*)

Will you tell me just what is going on?

BERO

Nothing, Old Man, nothing.

OLD MAN

I wish to write a letter.

68

**BERO**

Who to?

**OLD MAN**

To your superiors.

**BERO**

(*He winces, but recovers his poise.*)
There isn't such a thing.

**OLD MAN**

Your superiors, I said. I demand the right to send to them at once.
(*Pause.*)

**BERO** (*finally*)

You shall.

**OLD MAN**

I wish to write them at once. Now!

**BERO** (*turning to* AAFAA)

Fetch some writing material. Go to the nearest stationers.

**OLD MAN**

Why all the way to look for a store? Isn't there any in the house?

**BERO**

None that belongs to you. Perhaps you would give him money for your requirements?
(*The* OLD MAN *starts to take money from his pockets, slows down in suspicion, and looks at* BERO. *Then, slowly, he dips into all his trouser pockets.*)

**OLD MAN**

You know you took my money. Or ordered it removed.

**BERO**

I don't know anything of the sort.

69

OLD MAN (*violently*)

You know I have no money here!

BERO

I don't know anything. You on the contrary appear to know everything. Isn't that right? You know everything.
(*To* AAFAA.)
The Old Man appears to have no money. Obviously he can have no writing paper. Perhaps you would like to send a verbal message?

OLD MAN

You can take your verbal message to—
(*He looks at him scornfully, then sits down.*)

BERO

I tried to help. You will, of course, be given the best of everything you need. Need.
(*Pause.*)
Your food will get cold.

OLD MAN

I need my pipe.

BERO (*appearing to consider it*)

Why not? In this case I raise my idea of your need to coincide with your want.
(*He opens a cabinet, gives him his pipe and tobacco.*)
That gentleman there will offer you a light whenever you— need it.
(*The* OLD MAN *begins to stuff his pipe, normally at first, then slower and slower. When the pipe is filled he holds it by the bowl, waiting.* AAFAA *dips his hand in his pocket as if about to pull out matches, pauses, slowly holds out a closed fist, then opens it suddenly to reveal the hand empty. He breaks into silent laughter.*)

70

**OLD MAN**

I need a light.

**BERO**

And your watch. And glasses. And money. And paper. But do you really? I promised you the best of everything and this will prove to you I mean it.
(*He takes a packet of cigarettes from his pocket and offers it.*)
They are the best cigarettes on the market.
(*He takes out a packet of matches, holds out both matches and cigarettes in one hand, holds out the other hand, inviting him to return the pipe and tobacco.*)

**OLD MAN**

I prefer . . . my pipe.
(BERO *does not move. A long pause. The* OLD MAN *looks round at the* MENDICANTS *avidly watching. Finally he returns the pipe and pouch, accepts the cigarettes and matches, but moves the packet against his face to read the brand name.*

**BERO**

You can't see to read.
(*The* OLD MAN *snatches the box away from his face, opens the box and takes out a cigarette, lights it, then breaks into a slow smile.*)

**OLD MAN**

You would, wouldn't you? You would try that on me. Me! Shall I teach you what to say? Choice! Particularity! What redundant self-deceptive notions! More? More? Insistence on a floppy old coat, a rickety old chair, a moth-eaten hat which no certified lunatic would ever consider wearing, a car which breaks down twenty times in twenty minutes, an old idea riddled with the pellets of incidence. Enough? More? Are you cramming it up fast for the next victim? A perfect waterproof coat is rejected for a patched-up heirloom that gives the silly

wearer rheumatism. Is this an argument for freedom of choice? Is it sensible to cling so desperately to bits of the bitter end of a run-down personality? To the creak in an old chair, the crack in a cup, a crock of an old servant, the crick in the bottleneck of a man's declining years . . .
(*Pause. His voice changes.*)
But it did come to the test and I asked you all, what is one meat from another? Oh, your faces then, your faces . . .

BERO

You still boast of that? You go too far, Old Man.

OLD MAN

After all, what's meat for the ranks should be meat for the officers . . .
(*He chuckles.*)
It could happen, I said, it will happen. But I never really believed it.

BERO

They would have killed you, you know that? If I hadn't had you hidden away they would have killed you slowly.

OLD MAN (*still on his own*)

No. I've asked myself over and over again. I said it would happen, I knew it would happen, but I never really believed it.

BERO

They wanted to kill you, mutilate you, hang you upside down, then stuff your mouth with your own genitals. Did you know that?
(*His explosiveness breaks in on the* OLD MAN.)

OLD MAN

Why do you hesitate?

BERO

To do what?

72

OLD MAN

I said, why do you hesitate?
(*Pause.*)
Once you begin there is no stopping. You say, ah, this is the
last step, the highest step, but there is always one more step.
For those who want to step beyond, there is always one further
step.

BERO

Nothing more is needed.

OLD MAN

Oh yes, there is. I am the last proof of the human in you. The
last shadow. Shadows are tough things to be rid of.
(*He chuckles.*)
How does one prove he was never born of man? Of course you
could kill me . . .

BERO

Or you might just die . . .

OLD MAN

Quite possible, quite possible.

BERO

You're lucky you've lasted this far.

OLD MAN

I *have* lasted, but the question of being lucky . . . ?

BERO

There is a search for you everywhere.

OLD MAN

I thought that was over. Tenacious gods they worship, don't
they?

BERO

And you?

OLD MAN

Or maybe they are the tenacious gods.

BERO

And the god you worship?

OLD MAN

Abominates humanity—the fleshy part, that is.

BERO

Why As?

OLD MAN

Because Was—Is—Now . . .

BERO

Don't!

OLD MAN

So you see, I put you all beyond salvation.

BERO

Why As?

OLD MAN

A code. A word.

BERO

Why As?

OLD MAN

It had to be something.

BERO

Why As?

OLD MAN

If millions follow . . . that frightened you all.

BERO

Why As?

OLD MAN

Are you going to reopen the files? The case is closed. Insane, the verdict, thanks to you.

BERO

Why As?

OLD MAN

Why not?

BERO

Why As?

OLD MAN

Who wants to know?

BERO

I. Why As?

OLD MAN

What's in it for you?

BERO

*I* am asking questions! Why As?

OLD MAN

We went through this before.

BERO

I took a chance saving you.

OLD MAN

Risked your neck, yes. Compromised your position.

BERO

I didn't do that for nothing.

OLD MAN

It won't be for nothing. As my next-in-line you are my bene-ficiary. Legal. These of course are my natural heirs.

BERO

To what?

OLD MAN

As. What else?

BERO

I could turn you out and let them find you.

OLD MAN

The file is closed.

BERO

Is it? They are still looking for you.

OLD MAN

They should be looking for themselves. I robbed them of salvation.

BERO

Oh yes, you are good at quibbling.

OLD MAN

Oh, their faces! That was a picture. All those faces round the table.

BERO

If they hadn't been too surprised they would have shot you on the spot.

OLD MAN

Your faces, gentlemen, your faces. You should see your faces. And your mouths are hanging open. You're drooling but I am not exactly sure why. Is there really much difference? All intelligent animals kill only for food, you know, and you are intelligent animals. Eat-eat-eat-eat-eat—Eat!

BERO (*raises his arm*)

Stop it!

OLD MAN

(*He turns and holds him with his eyes.*)
Oh yes, you rushed out and vomited. You and the others. But
afterwards you said I had done you a favour. Remember?
(BERO *slowly lowers his arm.*)
I'm glad you remember. Never admit you are a recidivist once
you've tasted the favourite food of As.
(*Pause.*)

BERO

That's your last meal. Eat.
(BERO *begins to go out.*)

OLD MAN

Because it's *your* last chance?
(BERO *stops but doesn't turn round.*)
I guessed it. You have to prove you have not yourself been con-
taminated. But suppose you find no answer to take back, what
then?
(*Pause, smiling.*)
The—choice—is simple. *Be* contaminated!
(BERO *exits, slamming the door.*)

AAFAA

(*He dashes towards the food tray, opens the lid and sniffs.*)
Inspiration! C, Contentment. A full belly.
(*He starts to pick at the* OLD MAN's *food. The others join him,
wolfing down huge chunks of meat.* AAFAA *gnaws at a huge bone.*)
A full belly comes and goes; for half the people I know it never
comes. H—Humanity! Humanity the Ultimate Sacrifice to As,
the eternal oblation on the altar of As . . . I say, I get better
all the time!

GOYI (*irritated*)

At what? You're just a parrot.

77

AAFAA

I take exception to that. I'm a good pupil. The Old Man him-self admits it. The quickest of the underdogs, he always said.

GOYI

Yes, underdogs. First the Old Man tells us we are the underdogs, then his blasted son makes us his watchdogs!

AAFAA (*shrugs*)

Makes life a little more amusing you'll admit . . .

(*They continue to eat.*)

(BERO *and* SI BERO *meet in front of the house.*)

BERO

What is it? Are you spying on me?

SI BERO

What are you doing to him?

BERO

Keeping him safe. What do you imagine?

SI BERO

I wish to see him.

BERO

I've told you already . . .

SI BERO

I wish to see him.

BERO

You had your chance. No one can see him now.

SI BERO

Why not?

BERO

He's dangerous.

78

SI BERO

I'll risk it.

BERO

Infectious diseases are isolated. Nothing unusual about it, so stop making a fuss. I need to work in peace.

SI BERO

What am I to do? I have time on my hands. What can I do but think!

BERO

I've told you, leave the thinking to me. Stay in your little world and continue the work I set you.

SI BERO

That's over. And the old women no longer help. They sit and fold their arms.

BERO

I have no need of them. And you should never have brought them here. Throw them out.

SI BERO

They demand payment.

BERO

Then pay them off.

SI BERO

They won't take money.

BERO

So what do they want?

SI BERO

Nothing. But they refuse to leave until they are paid.

BERO (*looking in that direction*)

They are asking for death.

SI BERO

They don't seem to be afraid of you, Bero.

BERO

We shall see.
(*He turns to go towards the hut.*)

SI BERO

Wait, Bero, wait!

BERO

Well?

SI BERO

Don't harm them, Bero.

BERO

Either you throw them out or I will. Whose home is it? Theirs?
Do they now lay claim to the land?

SI BERO

It belongs to Father.

BERO

Forfeited. Legally, he does not exist.
(*He goes into the house.*
*In the clinic the* MENDICANTS *are picking at the last crumbs*
*of food, licking the last bone of its meat. One or two are hum-*
*ming the "Ballad of the Disabled." The* OLD MAN *reacts to the*
*sound of singing, listens, then turns away in disgust.*)

OLD MAN

I should have known better.

AAFAA (*stops*)

What, Old Man?

OLD MAN

For a moment I would have sworn I heard singing.

AAFAA

You heard us.

OLD MAN

I said singing, not cursing.

AAFAA

Perhaps you heard my spasms tuning up. It's like a set of wires, Old Man. Something touches them, they hum, and off I go.

OLD MAN

It doesn't bother you much these days, I notice.

AAFAA

That's true. They told me up there when it began, that it was something psy-cho-lo-gi-cal. Something to do with all the things happening around me, and the narrow escape I had. It's not so bad now. I still remember the first time. I was standing there just like this, blessing a group of six just about to go off. They were kneeling before me. Then—well, I can't say I heard the noise at all, because I was deaf for the next hour. So, this thing happened, no signal, no nothing. Six men kneeling in front of me, the next moment they were gone. Disappeared, just like that. That was when I began to shake. Nothing I could do to stop it. My back just went on bending over and snapping back again, like the spirit had taken me. God! What a way for the spirit to mount a man.

OLD MAN

But no revelations? No inspired pronouncements?

AAFAA (*angrily*)

What of you! I don't see you saving yourself in the situation you're in.
(*More to himself.*)
Or us.

OLD MAN.

There is nothing you can do, of course.

81

GOYI

Be fair, Old Man, how does a man cope with a situation like this? It was all right in the other place.

OLD MAN

So you find it different from the other places?

GOYI

It's not the same.

OLD MAN

There was no madness—then?
(*They react, silently.*)
You were not maimed then?
(*He holds up his hand to stop them.*)
And I mean, not merely in body. You were maimed then as now. You have lost the gift of self-disgust.

AAFAA

So have you, Old Man.

OLD MAN

Meaning?

CRIPPLE

I know what he means. I agree with him.

GOYI

So do I.

OLD MAN (*smiling*)

Explain. I do not understand.

CRIPPLE

You took the cigarette.

AAFAA

A man like me is letting himself down to say he is surprised by anything, but . . . I was surprised at you, Old Man. You may say I was a bit let down. We may be on opposite sides of the camp, but I like to see a man stand up for himself.

82

OLD MAN

Why?

AAFAA

So I can beat him down.
(*He guffaws, but no one joins him. He subsides.*)

OLD MAN

You were disgusted?

AAFAA (*soberly*)

More than.
(*The* OLD MAN *turns silently to each of them in turn.*)

CRIPPLE

Disappointed.

GOYI

Crucified.

OLD MAN

Disgust is cheap. I asked for self-disgust.

AAFAA

Yeah? You took the cigarette—what about that?

OLD MAN

Of course I did. Because I saw your faces.
(*He reaches in his pocket and throws towards them what turns out to be the barely smoked cigarette. All three pounce on it; the* CRIPPLE *comes out the winner.*)

AAFAA

Only one puff, only one, and then you pass it round.

OLD MAN

(*He watches them with contempt.*)
We'll go on that world tour yet. I'll take your circus round the world, so help me.

CRIPPLE (*slowly releasing a puff of smoke*)

Oh, that feels good. Haven't had such a good puff since that corpulent First Lady visited us and passed round imported cigarettes.

GOYI

The Old Man was mad for days. Suckers, he called us. Quite right too. Good smoke is a good suck. I wasn't going to throw away that superior brand just to please a crackpot.

AAFAA

Hey, remember the song the Old Man wrote to celebrate the occasion? Visit of the First Lady to the Home for the de-balled.

BLINDMAN

. . . for the Disabled.

AAFAA

Bloody pendant.

BLINDMAN

Pe-dant.

AAFAA (*gives up*)

Oh Christ!

CRIPPLE (*singing*)

He came smelling of wine and roses, wine and roses

MENDICANTS

. . . wine and roses.

(AAFAA *gradually warms up towards his spastic dance.*)

CRIPPLE

He came smelling of wine and roses.
On his arm his wife was gushpillating . . .

BLINDMAN

Palpitating.

AAFAA

Oh, can't you shut up? Don't mind him, start all over again.

84

CRIPPLE

He came smelling of wine and roses.
On his arm his wife was gushpillating, gushpillating . . .

MENDICANTS

. . . gushpillating.
(*The singing fades out.* BERO *comes out of the house, holstering a revolver. He goes up to the* OLD WOMEN's *hut quietly and tries to peep inside.* IYA AGBA *leans out of the hut and speaks almost directly in his ear.*)

IYA AGBA

Does the specialist have time for a word or two?
(BERO *is startled, leaps aside.*)
Did I scare you?

BERO

(*He recovers, looks her over carefully.*)
What is a thing like you still doing alive?

IYA AGBA

Can we help you?

BERO

Do what? Just pack up and get out of here before morning.

IYA AGBA

We can help you cure him.

BERO

Who?

IYA AGBA

He's sick, that is what we heard.

BERO

You heard wrong. I am giving you warning to clear out of here.
Pick up your lice and rags and get out.

IYA AGBA

Is anyone else sick that we know of?

85

BERO

By tomorrow I want you out.

IYA AGBA

We want to help him.

BERO

No one needs help from you. Now get out of my way.

IYA AGBA

Maybe you do.

BERO

Do I have to fling you aside!

IYA AGBA (*standing aside*)

Pass, then.
(*She lets him take a few steps, then.*)
Your sister owes us a debt.

BERO

(*He stops, turns slowly.*)
If you know what is good for you, you will never let me hear
that again.

IYA AGBA

We took her into the fold—did she tell you that? To teach what
we know, a pupil must come into the fold.

BERO

What fold? Some filthy thieving cult?

IYA AGBA

It's no light step for man or woman.

BERO

And what . . . cult is this?

IYA AGBA

Not any cult you can destroy. We move as the Earth moves,
nothing more. We age as Earth ages.

86

**BERO**

But you're afraid to tell me the name.

**IYA AGBA**

I try to keep fools from temptation.

**BERO** (*instantly angry*)

Watch it, old woman, your age earns no privileges with me.

**IYA AGBA**

Nothing does, from what we hear. So you want to know what cult, do you?

**BERO**

I can ask your—pupil.
(*He turns round to go back to his house.*)

**IYA AGBA**

She won't tell you. Take it from me. She won't.
(BERO *stops without turning, waits.*)
Your mind has run farther than the truth. I see it searching, going round and round in darkness. Truth is always too simple for a desperate mind.

**BERO** (*going*)

I shall find out.

**IYA AGBA**

Don't look for the sign of broken bodies or wandering souls. Don't look for the sound of fear or the smell of hate. Don't take a bloodhound with you; we don't mutilate bodies.

**BERO**

Don't teach me my business.

**IYA AGBA**

If you do, you may find him circle back to your door.

**BERO**

Watch your mouth, old hag.

IYA AGBA

You want the name? But how much would it tell you, young man? We put back what we take, in one form or another. Or more than we take. It's the only law. What laws do you obey?

BERO

You are proscribed, whatever you are, you are banned.

IYA AGBA

What can that mean? You'll proscribe Earth itself? How does one do that?

BERO

I offer you a last chance.

IYA AGBA

The fool is still looking for names. How much would it tell you?

BERO

You'll find out when they come for you.

IYA AGBA

What will you step on, young fool? Even on the road to damnation a man must rest his foot somewhere.

(BERO *marches furiously back to the clinic. He is stopped at the door by the sound coming from the clinic. He listens.*)

CRIPPLE

. . . On his arm his wife was gushpillating, gushpillating . . .

MENDICANTS

. . . gushpillating . . .

CRIPPLE

You never saw such a gushpillating wife
Oh, was it gross and was it ugly, was it ugly . . .

MENDICANTS

. . . was it ugly . . .

CRIPPLE

That thing he had clinging onto his arm
And she knew that all the men did think so, men did
think so . . .

MENDICANTS

                   . . . men did think so . . .

CRIPPLE

Did find their own predicaments much prettier.
So she looked them mean and smiled them dirty,
smiled them dirty . . .

MENDICANTS

              . . . smiled them dirty . . .

CRIPPLE

And her mouth formed silent words
I may be gross but dears, I'm not beyond it, not
beyond it . . .

MENDICANTS

                 . . . not beyond it . . .

CRIPPLE

I may be old but not beyond it.
While you according to diagnosis, diagnosis . . .

MENDICANTS

                 . . . diagnosis . . .

CRIPPLE

Will ne . . . ver . . .
(*He pauses, splutters as if trying to control his mirth, which
finally breaks out fully. The* MENDICANTS *join in, then at a
rallying signal from* AAFAA, *control themselves long enough to
end—*)

ALL

           . . . hm-hm-hm . . . no more.

89

AAFAA

That was the best song you ever wrote for us, Old Man. Ballad of the State Visit to the Home of the De-balled.

CRIPPLE

I prefer the second one.

GOYI

Which one?

CRIPPLE

Pro patria mourir.

MENDICANTS

. . . mourir mourir mourir . . .

CRIPPLE

Dulce et decorum . . .

MENDICANTS

. . . quorum quorum quorum . . .

OLD MAN

Corum, stupes, not quorum.

MENDICANTS

Corum corum corum, not quorum.

OLD MAN

Decorum. Dulce et decorum . . .

MENDICANTS

. . . quorum quorum quorum . . .

OLD MAN

God damn you. Can you learn nothing?—corum, not quorum.

GOYI

No quorum, no quorum, that's the damned trouble.

CRIPPLE

Yes sir, you've banged the hammer on the nail.

OLD MAN (*turning to* AAFAA)

Will you tell me what these idiots are talking about?

AAFAA

They've lost me.

CRIPPLE

You've gone dense.
(*Quoting the* OLD MAN *again.*)
In ancient Athens . . .

AAFAA

Damn it, you're right. No damned quorum!

BLINDMAN

In ancient Athens they didn't just have a quorum. Everybody was there! That, children, was democracy.

CRIPPLE (*singing, to the tune of "When the Saints Go Marching In"*)
Before I join
The saints above
Before I join
The saints above
I want to sit on that damned quorum
Before I join the saints above

Before I bid
This earth adieu
Before I bid
This earth adieu
I want my dues from that damned quorum
Before I bid this earth adieu
(*The others join in, drumming on the floor, table, etc., with their crutches, knuckles, etc., repeating the chorus. "I want my dues . . . Before adieus," in place of "Oh when the saints . . . go marching in."*

*As the tempo warms up* BERO *enters.*)

BERO (*entering*)

So you haven't given up your little tricks.

OLD MAN

Does it bother you?

BERO

No. It is bad for you, though.

OLD MAN

It seems to interest you. Spend more time with us.

BERO

What gives you that idea?

OLD MAN

I could hear you listening outside. You were fascinated.

BERO

My interest in you is strictly . . .

OLD MAN

That of a specialist. Proceed.

BERO

How did you do it?

OLD MAN

Do what?

BERO

No more evasions. How did you do it? What made you do it?

OLD MAN

Prod. Prod. Probe. Probe. Don't you know yet what I am?
(*Dramatic whisper.*)
Octopus. Plenty of reach but nothing to seize on. I re-create my
tentacles, so cut away.

BERO

To me you are simply another organism, another mould or
strain under the lens. Sometimes a strain proves malignant and

it becomes dangerous to continue with it. In such a case there is only one thing to do.

OLD MAN

Are you equipped for that here?

BERO

Even I have no control over accidents. Just now I came through that room of herbs, I saw something I recognized.

OLD MAN

Something to sap the mind? Or destroy it altogether?

BERO

It depends on the dose. I brought you some.

(*He brings some berries from his pockets and drops them gently over the* OLD MAN'*s head.*)

If you ever get tired and you feel you need a nightcap like a certain ancient Greek you were so fond of quoting, just soak a handful of them in water.

OLD MAN

You've used it before, haven't you? Or something similar. I saw your victims, afterwards.

BERO

They were provided a Creed, but they talked heresy. Same as you.

OLD MAN

Creed? Heresy? Bread, pleurisy and what next? Will you try and speak some intelligible language.

BERO

They corrupted unformed minds. That was ba-a-ad.

OLD MAN

Unformed minds in deformed bodies.

BERO

Again you are being evasive.

OLD MAN

I asked to be sent where I would do the most good. I was and I did.

BERO (*smiling*)

I also was sent where I would do the most good. I was and I did.
(*Pause.*)
It would appear that we were both efficient volunteers.
(*Again, pause.*)
What exactly is As, Old Man?

OLD MAN

As?

BERO

You know As, the playword of your convalescents, the pivot of whatever doctrine you used to confuse their minds, your piffling battering ram at the idealism and purpose of this time and history. What is As, Old Man?

OLD MAN

You seem to have described it to your satisfaction.

BERO

(*Thundering, moving suddenly, he passes his swagger stick across the* OLD MAN'*s throat, holding it from behind and pressing.*)
I'm asking you! What is As? Why As!

OLD MAN

(*He gasps but tries to smile. He cranes up to look him in the face.*)
In a way I should be flattered. You want to borrow my magic key. Yours open only one door at a time.

BERO

WHY AS!

94

OLD MAN

And rusty? Bent? Worn? Poisonous? When you're through the lock is broken? The room empty?

BERO

What is As?

OLD MAN

But why? Do you want to set up shop against me? Or against . . . others?
(*He rolls his eyes towards the* MENDICANTS.)
I think we have a conspiracy.

BERO

What is As?

OLD MAN

As Was, Is, Now, As Ever Shall be . . .

BERO (*in a tone of quiet menace*)

Don't play with me, Old Man.

OLD MAN

As doesn't change.

BERO (*increasing pressure*)

From what? To what?

OLD MAN

(*He chokes, tugs at the swagger stick.* BERO *lets go. The* OLD MAN *gets up, chafing his neck.*)
Do you know what one of those men once said? Let's send our gangrenous dressings by post to those sweet-smelling As agencies and homes. He sat down to compile a mailing list.

BERO

Yes?

OLD MAN

I understood.

BERO

What did you understand?

OLD MAN

As.

BERO

(*He has a violent reaction, then controls himself.*)
You are certified insane. Your fate creates no anxiety in anyone. Take a look at your companions—your humanity.

OLD MAN

I recognized it. A part of me identifies with every human being.

BERO

You'll be disillusioned soon enough.

OLD MAN

I do not harbour illusions. You do.

BERO (*genuinely astonished*)

I? You say that of me. I, of all people?

OLD MAN

Oh, you are in good company. Even the cripple who is down to earth harbours illusions. Now, that's strange. I would have thought you would find that funny.

BERO

I do not need illusions. I control lives.

OLD MAN

Control—lives? What does that mean? Tell me what is the experience of it. Is it a taste? A smell? A feel? Do you have a testament that vindicates?

BERO

We have nothing that a petty mind can grasp.
(*Pause.*)
Try if you can, Old Man, to avoid twitching. Control belongs only to a few with the aptitude.

OLD MAN

One should always expect something new from the specialist.
(*Contemptuously.*)
Control!

BERO

Your old games won't help you. Forget that line.

OLD MAN

Throw me a new line then. Feed the drowning man a line.

BERO

You can swim.

OLD MAN (*turning to the others*)

See? He's getting good. Swim? How?

BERO (*viciously*)

We'll flood the place for you.

OLD MAN (*pleased*)

You're getting very good, very good. It catches, you see. How
do I swim? We'll flood the place. Or . . . is it merely in char-
acter? Is that it? Your peculiar little specialization. Perhaps that's
it. So. When do you start?

BERO

Perhaps not at all. It would take too long.

OLD MAN (*nodding*)

Y-e-s. And the place is not waterproof. I noticed rats. That
means holes. You should see the rats.

BERO

They'll desert.

OLD MAN (*gazing round at the* MENDICANTS)

I suppose so.

BERO

Or smoke you out. You will suffocate, slowly.

OLD MAN

Smoke. Smoke-screen. That's what it all is.

BERO

What?

OLD MAN

The pious pronouncements. Manifestos. Charades. At the bottom of it all humanity choking in silence.

BERO

You think a lot of yourself, don't you?

OLD MAN

Who else shall I think much of? You?

BERO

I control . . .

OLD MAN (*waves it aside*)

Tell me something new. Or if you won't, these ones will. Aafaa!

AAFAA

What now?

OLD MAN

We are done with the flood. It never came. These midgets try to re-create the Flood, but they lack the power. At least God had a reason. A damnable reason, but at least he had a reason. And a good pump to clean up the mess. Not like these. What do you offer in place of the Flood?

AAFAA (*challenging*)

Running water.

OLD MAN (*in a disgusted tone*)

Nothing better?

AAFAA

You're dodging.

98

OLD MAN

Running water!
(*He turns to the* CRIPPLE.)
You deal with that. It's beneath my intellect.

CRIPPLE

Muddy. How do I get across it?

OLD MAN

God, they're all so self-centred. He means running progress.
Faucets, pipes.

CRIPPLE

Can't reach the tap. Too high.

AAFAA

And who cares about you? Just who the hell do you think you
are?

CRIPPLE (*stubbornly*)

Too high.

OLD MAN (*smiles*)

Like the price. See? Blindman?

BLINDMAN

Running water? Running mouths. Election promises.

OLD MAN (*to* BERO)

See? Let's have a new one.

AAFAA

Electricity.
(*Seeing* BLINDMAN *about to speak.*)
And don't you tell me it's no good to you.

BLINDMAN

And whose fault is that? I wasn't born blind, you know.

CRIPPLE

Ho, ho, remember that story of the blind man with a lamp?

GOYI

Don't tell me you went to school too?

AAFAA

What! Same old primer? Reader II or . . . was it Reader III?

CRIPPLE (*complacently*)

Reader III, Elementary. Lamb and Wool Reader for Schools—well, something like that.

AAFAA

I bet you stopped at III.

CRIPPLE

No. Went up to four. Then I got the call of the road.

GOYI

I'll tell the story. A blind man went walking one day, carrying a lamp. Thereupon he met a neighbour. The neighbour stared, amazed . . .

AAFAA

A born fool.

CRIPPLE

I bet you would have found it queer too.

AAFAA

You forget I am a student of human peculiarities. Human peculiarities.

GOYI

Shut up, let me continue.

AAFAA

The neighbour said, Good blind neighbour, what good on earth is a lamp to you?

GOYI

Whereupon the blind man replied . . .

ALL TOGETHER (*in kindergarten voice*)

I carry this lamp, good fellow, not that I may see but . . .
(*Pause.*)

AAFAA

So that the whole world can see you when you try to rob me.
(*He bursts into his maniacal laughter, joined by the others.*)

OLD MAN (*reflectively*)

A lamp has its uses.

AAFAA

So, electricity.

GOYI

Bleeah! Election promises.

CRIPPLE

What we want is individual manifestos.

AAFAA

Manifesto for every freak? General Electric!

OLD MAN

Electrocutes. Electric chair. Electrodes on the nerve centres—
your favourite pastime, I believe? Tell me something new. What
hasn't been abused?

BERO

(*He has taken out his gun, weighs it significantly.*)
And lightning strikes. What about it?

OLD MAN

The boy learns. The boy learns.

BERO

Don't you dare patronize me. Answer me, what about it?

OLD MAN

That lightning strikes? It could strike you, no?

BERO

Yes.

OLD MAN (*with a quiet, triumphant smile*)

Then you're not omnipotent. You can't do a flood and you—
(*Pause.*)
—can't always dodge lightning. Why do you ape the nonexistent one who can? Why do you ape nothing?

BERO

You tax my patience. Better watch out in future.

OLD MAN (*quietly*)

The future?

BERO

The future, yes. The End . . .

OLD MAN

Justifies the meanness.

BERO

(*Again, he has an angry reaction. He controls himself.*)
Just think of this—you have none.

OLD MAN (*calling after him*)

Tell me something new. Tell me what is happening in the future.
(*They all listen to* BERO's *footsteps receding.*)
If he'd waited, I would have told him what's happening in the future. A faithful woman picking herbs for a smoke-screen on abuse.
(*Lights come up sharply in the* OLD WOMEN's *hut. No break in action.*)

IYA AGBA (*screaming*)

Abuse! Abuse! What do we do? Close our eyes and see nothing?

IYA MATE

Patience now. Patience.

IYA AGBA

What is it then! I see abominations. What do you see?

IYA MATE

The same, but . . .

IYA AGBA

Then what are we waiting for? Get ready the pot of fire.

IYA MATE

Do you think a little more time . . . ?

IYA AGBA

To do worse? To do more? It's a good night for settling accounts.

IYA MATE

She's a good woman.

IYA AGBA

Get it ready. Get it ready. I'll not be a tool in their hands, not in this ripe state—No! Too much has fallen in their hands already, it's time to take it back. They spat on my hands when I held them out bearing gifts. Have you ever known it different?

IYA MATE

We hoped this might be.

IYA AGBA

Hope is dead, I must defend what is mine. Or let it die also. Let it be destroyed.

IYA MATE

Everything?

IYA AGBA

Everything. Everything they took from me.

IYA MATE

I think only of her.

IYA AGBA

She's a good woman and her heart is strong. And it is that kind who tire suddenly in their sleep and pass on to join their ancestors. What happens then?

IYA MATE

We can wait till then.

IYA AGBA

And I? Have you spoken to the ones below, and did they tell you I shall still be among the living when her bones are rested?

IYA MATE

You leave me nothing to say.

IYA AGBA

There is nothing more to say. We pay our dues to earth in time, I also take back what is mine.
(*The clinic as last seen. Instant transition as before.*)

CRIPPLE (*singing*)

I want my dues
Not promises
I want my dues
Not promises . . .

AAFAA (*singing*)

I want my dues.
(*Stops.*)
How about it, Old Man? I want my world tour. Old Man, you promised. I want that world tour you promised.

CRIPPLE

Promises. What else have we ever got from him?

GOYI

He got us the cigarettes anyway.

104

AAFAA

Raises a man's hopes for nothing. So where is this world tour you kept promising?

CRIPPLE

A Travelling Exhibition of As Grotesques, I remember.

AAFAA

You should, you illiterate reptile. You flung your crutches at his head because you thought it was an insult didn't you? Said he was making fun of you.

CRIPPLE

Why bring it up? The Blindman explained it. He said Grotesque only meant Greatest and I said I was sorry.

GOYI

He did too, I remember. And the Old Man also promised me top billing.
(*Pause.*)
I didn't want to ask at the time, but what is top billing, Blindman?

AAFAA

It means the Old Man would see that you got to the top of the ladder.
(*Pause.*)

CRIPPLE

How do *I* get there, Aafaa?

AAFAA

Why ask me foolish questions, you persistent little egotist? When the specialist told you you'd soon be doing better than you were when you had both legs, did you come to Aafaa for explanations?

GOYI

So? Are we getting the world tour or not?

CRIPPLE

Nitwit! As if he could even do anything about that now. Better forget it.

AAFAA

Old Man, you shouldn't have promised the travelling show.
(*Changing voice.*)
Beat all known circuses hollow. I'll take the wrappings off you and leave the world gasping. What else . . . ?

CRIPPLE

You've been pushed in the background too often.

GOYI

Always hidden away.

CRIPPLE (*coyly*)

Not that we're shy.

GOYI

Always hidden away.

CRIPPLE

We're more decent than most. Hn-hn, than most.

AAFAA

Hidden under pension schemes you are.

GOYI

Tail-of-the-parade outings.

AAFAA

Behind the big drum.

CRIPPLE

Under royalty visits.

AAFAA (*graciously proffering his hand*)

You may.
(GOYI *kisses his hand.*)

CRIPPLE

Imperial commendations.

(AAFAA *unfurls the scrolls, slaps his tongue up and down.*)

CRIPPLE

Unveiling of the plaque . . .

GOYI

Commemoration occasion . . .

AAFAA

Certificates of merit . . .

GOYI

Long-service medals . . .

(*The* CRIPPLE *dashes forward to the feet of* AAFAA, *who takes medals from an invisible aide. His eyes roll from side to side, seeing no one.* GOYI *goes to him, taps him and points to the* CRIPPLE. AAFAA *tries but cannot make it. Finally he kisses* GOYI *on both cheeks, who then kisses the* CRIPPLE *on both cheeks. He pins the medal on* GOYI'*s left shoulder, who then pins medal on the* CRIPPLE'*s chest. All three cry: "Speech" "Speech" "We want Him" "We want Him" "We want Him" rising to a crescendo. Finally* BLINDMAN *gets up, walks slowly downstage.*)

BLINDMAN

(*The speech should be varied with the topicality and locale of the time.*)

It was our duty and a historical necessity. It is our duty and a historical beauty. It shall always be. What we have, we hold. What though the wind of change is blowing over this entire continent, our principles and traditions—yes, must be maintained. For we are threatened, yes, we are indeed threatened. Excuse me, please, but we are entitled to match you history for history to the nearest half-million souls. Look at the hordes, I implore you. They stink. They eat garlic. What on earth have we in common with *them?* Understand me, please, understand me and do not misinterpret my intentions. The copper is quite incidental. Manganese? I don't know what it means. I always thought it was female for Kantagese. As for oil, I can't tell which is the margarine. If we don't stop them now, who knows but it may be our turn next moment. I ask you, do you want to wake up murdered in your beds?

(*The others laugh.*)

I assure you it's quite possible. No, please, it's no laughing matter. I mean . . . oh, I beg your pardon. You know what I mean, of course, do you want to wake up and find you've been . . . no I suppose that is also unlikely; better simply say . . . oh, well, look, strictly between you and me, all it boils down to is—would you want your daughter married to one of them? . . . It may happen, believe me, it may happen—if we're lucky. Rape is more natural to them than marriage. Even Confucius said it—if it must be, lie back and enjoy it. That coming from their greatest—er—er—atomic scientist is not a statement to be taken lightly. The black menace is no figment of my father's imagination. Look here . . . have you had the experience of watching them—breed? No no, I mean . . . I don't mean being actually *there* . . . please please please, I was referring to statistics, statistics. We feed those statistics into a computer and here is what they say . . . What we have, we hold. What though the wind of change is blowing over this entire continent, our principles and traditions—yes, must be maintained. For we are threatened. Yes, we are indeed threatened. Excuse me, but we are entitled to match you history for history to the nearest half-million souls. Look at the hordes, I implore you. They stink. They eat garlic . . .

(*As* BLINDMAN *begins the re-run, the other* MENDICANTS *commence their chant,* AAFAA *taking the lead. The song goes faster and faster and louder and they clap him down until* BLINDMAN *gives up and bows.*)

108

As Is Was Now
As Ever Shall Be

Bi o ti wa    etc. etc.
Ni yi o se wa
Bi o ti wa
Ni yi o se wa
(*They give* BLINDMAN *a round of applause while he feels his way towards the* OLD MAN.)

BLINDMAN

I hope I didn't do too badly.

OLD MAN

(*He sighs, turns to face him.*)
No. It was quite a good effort.

BLINDMAN

It was rather like old times.

OLD MAN

Very much like old times.

CRIPPLE

Hey, listen. The Old Man was pleased.

AAFAA

I should bloody well hope so. It was just like old times.

CRIPPLE

My feelings exactly. Just like old times.

GOYI

It . . . was . . . just . . . like old times.

AAFAA

Yes. So why risk putting us here together?

OLD MAN

Because . . . we are together in As.
(*He rises slowly.*)

As Is, and the System is its mainstay though it wear a hundred masks and a thousand outward forms. And because you are within the System, the cyst in the System that irritates, the foul gurgle of the cistern, the expiring function of a faulty cistern and are part of the material for reformulating the mind of a man into the necessity of the moment's political As, the moment's scientific As, metaphysic As, sociologic As, economic, re-creative ethical As, you-cannot-es-cape! There is but one constant in the life of the System and that constant is AS. And what can you pit against the priesthood of that constant deity, its gospellers, its enforcement agency. And even if you say unto them, do I not know you, did I not know you in rompers, with leaky nose and smutty face? Did I not know you thereafter, know you in the haunt of cat-houses, did I not know you rifling the poor-boxes in the local church, did I not know you dissolving the night in fumes of human self-indulgence simply simply simply did I not know you, do you not defecate, fornicate, prevaricate when heaven and earth implore you to abdicate and are you not prey to headaches, indigestion, colds, disc displacement, ingrowing toenail, dysentery, malaria, flatfoot, corns and chilblains. Simply simply, do I not know you Man like me? Then shall they say unto you, I am chosen, restored, redesignated and redestined and further further shall they say unto you, you heresiarchs of the System arguing questioning querying weighing puzzling insisting rejecting upon you all shall we practise, without passion—

MENDICANTS

Practise . . .

OLD MAN

With no ill-will . . .

MENDICANTS

Practise . . .

OLD MAN

With good conscience . . .

MENDICANTS

Practise . . .

OLD MAN

That the end shall . . .

MENDICANTS

Practise . . .

OLD MAN

Justify the meanness . . .

MENDICANTS

Practise . . .

OLD MAN

Without emotion . . .

MENDICANTS

Practise . . .

OLD MAN

Without human ties . . .

MENDICANTS

Practise . . .

OLD MAN

Without—no—Lest there be self-doubting . . .

MENDICANTS

Practise . . . As Was the Beginning, As Is, Now, As Ever Shall Be, World Without.

(*As the* OLD MAN *slowly resumes his seat,* AAFAA *rises, speaking.*)

AAFAA

In the beginning was the Priesthood, and the Priesthood was one. Then came schism after schism by a parcel of schismatic ticks in the One Body of Priesthood, the political priesthood went right the spiritual priesthood went left or vice versa the political priesthood went back the spiritual priesthood went fore and vice versa the political priesthood went down the spiritual priesthood went up or vice versa the loyalty of homo sapiens was never divided for two parts of a division make a whole and there was no hole in the monolithic solidarity of two halves of the priesthood. No, there was no division. The loyalty of homo sapiens regressed into himself, himself his little tick-tock self, self-ticking, self-tickling, self-tackling problems that belonged to the priesthood spiritual and political while they remained the sole and indivisible one. Oh, look at him, Monsieur l'homme sapiens, look at the lone usurper of the ancient rights and privileges of the priesthood—

(*The* CRIPPLE *makes an obscene gesture.* AAFAA *registers shock.*)
—look at the dog in dogma raising his hindquarters to cast the scent of his individuality on the lamppost of Destiny! On him practise. Practise! Practise! As was the Beginning—

MENDICANTS

Practise . . .

AAFAA

As Is . . .

MENDICANTS

Practise . . .

AAFAA

Now . . .

MENDICANTS

Practise . . .

AAFAA

As Ever Shall Be . . .

MENDICANTS

Practise . . .

AAFAA

World without . . .

MENDICANTS

Practise! Practise! Practise!
(*From the chorus of "Practise" they slip into their chant, softly.*)

OLD MAN (*rising again*)

On the cyst in the system, you cysts, you damnable warts . . .
(*He freezes with his arm raised towards the next scene as if in benediction.*

*The "Bi o ti wa" chant continues underneath and* AAFAA *continues with his spastic dance somewhat muted all through the next scene.*

IYA AGBA *and* IYA MATE *have arrived in front of* SI BERO'*s house, the latter carrying the pot of glowing coals. She places it on the ground.*)

IYA AGBA

Call her name.

IYA MATE

Si Bero!
(SI BERO *comes out a few moments later, obviously roused from sleep. She notices first the pot of coals, then makes out figures of the two women in the dark. She shrinks back.*)
Don't be afraid, daughter. No harm will come to you.

IYA AGBA

We thought it was time for a visit. Bid us welcome so we can go about our business.

SI BERO

It's . . . it's an unusual time for earth-mothers to visit their daughters.

IYA AGBA

Not if they have debts to collect. Say how you want it done, woman.

SI BERO

Debts! No, not him. Don't touch him, my mothers.

IYA AGBA

I waste no strength on carrion. I leave him to earth's rejection.

SI BERO

Give me more time. I have the power of a mother with him.

IYA MATE (*gently*)

We waited as long as we could, daughter.

IYA AGBA

Time has run out. Do you think time favours us? Can I sleep easy when my head is gathering mould on your shelves?

SI BERO

You said yourself nothing goes to waste.

IYA AGBA

What is used for evil is also put to use. Have I not sat with the knowledge of abuse these many days and kept the eyes of my mind open?

IYA MATE

It cannot wait, daughter. Evil hands soon find a use for the best of things.

SI BERO

Let it wait, my mothers, let it wait.

IYA AGBA (*angrily*)

Rain falls and seasons turn. Night comes and goes—do you think they wait for the likes of you? I warned you when we took you in the fold . . .

SI BERO

I'll repay it all, I promise . . .

IYA AGBA

I said this gift is not one you gather in one hand. If your other hand is fouled the first withers also.

**IYA MATE**

That is how we met it. No one can change that.

SI BERO (*clutching* IYA MATE *around the knees*)

Not you too. You were never as hard as she.

**IYA MATE**

Nothing we can do, daughter, nothing but follow the way as we met it.

**SI BERO**

And the good that is here? Does that count for nothing?

**IYA AGBA**

We'll put that into the test. Let us see how it takes to fire.

**SI BERO**

Fire?

**IYA AGBA**

It is only the dying embers of an old woman's life. The dying embers of earth as we knew it. Is that anything to fear?

**SI BERO**

We laboured hard together.

**IYA AGBA**

So does the earth on which I stand. And on which your house stands, woman. If you want the droppings of rodents on your mat I can only look on. But my head still fills your room from wall to wall and dirty hands touch it . . .

**SI BERO**

No, no, nobody but myself . . .

**IYA AGBA**

I need to sleep in peace . . .
(*She raises the pot suddenly to throw the embers into the stove.* BERO *steps out at that moment, gun in hand, bearing down on* IYA AGBA.)

OLD MAN

*(His voice has risen to a frenzy.)*
Practise, Practise, Practise . . . on the cyst in the system . . .
(BERO *is checked in stride by the voice. He now hesitates between the two distractions.)*
. . . you cyst, you cyst, you splint in the arrow of arrogance, the dog in dogma, tick of a heretic, the tick in politics, the mock of democracy, the mar of marxism, a tic of the fanatic, the boo in buddhism, the ham in Mohammed, the dash in the criss-cross of Christ, a dot on the i of ego an ass in the mass, the ash in ashram, a boot in kibbutz, the pee of priesthood, the peepee of perfect priesthood, oh how dare you raise your hindquarters you dog of dogma and cast the scent of your existence on the lamppost of Destiny you HOLE IN THE ZERO of NOTHING!

CRIPPLE

I have a question.

OLD MAN

*(He turns slowly towards the interruption.)*
It's the dreamer.

CRIPPLE

I have a question.

OLD MAN

Black that Zero!
(AAFAA, GOYI *and* BLINDMAN *begin to converge on the* CRIPPLE.)

CRIPPLE

I have a question.

OLD MAN

Shut that gaping hole or we fall through it.

CRIPPLE

I have a question.

116

(*The* MENDICANTS' *chorus "Practise" as they beat him.*)

OLD MAN

Stop him cold, stop him dead! Let me hear the expiring suction of an imperfect system.

CRIPPLE

My question is . . .
(AAFAA *snatches one of* GOYI's *crutches. In the background the sound of* BERO *breaking down the door.* AAFAA *brings down crutch on the* CRIPPLE's *head.*)

OLD MAN

Stop him! Fire! Fire! Riot! Hot line! Armageddon!
(*As he shouts, the* OLD MAN *snatches the surgeon's coat from where it is hanging, puts it on, dons cap, pulls on the gloves, and picks up a scalpel.*)

OLD MAN (*at the top of his voice*)

Bring him over here.
(*He dons mask.*)
Bring him over here. Lay him out. Stretch him flat. Strip him bare. Bare! Bare! Bare his soul! Light the stove!
(*They heave him onto the table and hold him down while the* OLD MAN *rips the shirt open to bare the* CRIPPLE's *chest.* BERO *rushes in and takes in the scene, raises his pistol, and aims at the* OLD MAN.)

OLD MAN

Let us taste just what makes a heretic tick.
(*He raises the scalpel in a motion for incision.* BERO *fires. The* OLD MAN *spins, falls face upwards on the table as the* CRIPPLE *slides to the ground from under him. A momentary freeze on stage. Then* SI BERO *rushes from the* OLD WOMEN *towards the clinic. Instantly* IYA AGBA *hurls the embers into the stove, and thick smoke belches out from the doorway, gradually filling out the stage. Both women walk calmly away as* SI BERO *reappears in*

*the doorway of the clinic. The* MENDICANTS *turn to look at her, break gleefully into their favourite song. The* OLD WOMEN *walk past their hut, stop at the spot where the* MENDICANTS *were first seen, and look back towards the clinic. The song stops in mid-word and the lights snap out simultaneously.*)
Bi o ti wa
Ni yio se wa

Bi o ti wa

Ni yio se wa
Bi o ti wa l'atete ko.